PUPPY IN A PRESENT

"Well, now that you have one, you'd better keep in mind that it's your puppy, not mine," said Mrs. Benn. "And that means feeding her, cleaning up after her, taking her out for a walk before you go to school and again when you come home, brushing her. . . ."

"I know, I know." Chloe sighed, sounding impatient.

"Training her, too," Mandy couldn't resist adding. She knew that well-behaved dogs stood a much better chance of having a permanent home than dogs who'd had no guidance from their owners and so ended up being a nuisance.

PUPPY in a PRESENT

Ben M. Baglio

Illustrations by Ann Baum

Cover illustration by
Mary Ann Lasher

AN
APPLE
PAPERBACK

SCHOLASTIC INC.
New York Toronto London Auckland Sydney
Mexico City New Delhi Hong Kong Buenos Aires

Special thanks to Andrea Abbott

ISBN 0-439-68759-4

Text copyright © 2004 by Working Partners Limited.
Created by Working Partners Limited, London W6 0QT.
Illustrations copyright © 2004 by Ann Baum.

12 11 10 9 8 7 6 5 4 3 2 1   4 5 6 7 8 9/0

Printed in the U.S.A.   40
First Scholastic printing, November 2004

One

"Hey, great Christmas tree!" Mandy Hope exclaimed when she and her mom drove up outside the doctor's office in Welford on a frosty morning two weeks before Christmas.

The dark green fir tree grew in the middle of Dr. Mason's front yard. For most of the year it looked quite ordinary, but it had been transformed overnight with strings of colored lights so that it glowed and sparkled even in the pale morning sunshine.

"Dr. Mason must have spent half the night decorating it," Mandy added, opening her door and climbing out of the Land Rover.

1

Dr. Emily Hope took the keys out of the ignition and put them in her coat pocket. "He's certainly done a good job. This is one of the best Christmas trees I've seen so far this year."

"Maybe it's a way of cheering up people who aren't feeling very well," Mandy suggested.

"Could be," her mom agreed. "It's bound to take people's minds off feeling sick, even for a moment."

Unlike most people who walked past the tree, Mandy and her mom weren't there because they were unwell. Instead, they'd come to check on Dr. Mason's pet rats, Jigsaw and Puzzle, who had developed eye infections. Dr. Emily, who was a vet, had diagnosed the problem yesterday and this morning she and Mandy were bringing some special eyedrops to reduce the swelling and tackle the infection.

"I'm glad we had to come back today," Mandy said, going up the short flight of stairs to the front door. She patted her pocket to make sure the dropper bottle containing the medicine was still there.

Emily Hope smiled at her. "Let me guess. It's not just because of the stunning tree, is it? You're dying to handle those rats again."

Mandy smiled back. "How did you guess?"

"I have no idea," said Dr. Emily, pretending to look

baffled. "Perhaps it's got something to do with you being just a little bit crazy about animals."

"I'm not a little bit crazy about animals. I'm *a lot* crazy about them!" Mandy laughed. She wasn't exaggerating. To her, animals were more important than anything else. And luckily for twelve-year-old Mandy, her mom and dad ran Animal Ark, a veterinary clinic that was attached to their home in the small Yorkshire village of Welford. Living at Animal Ark meant she'd already learned a lot about treating sick animals. Now it was Jigsaw and Puzzle's turn to teach her something about eye infections in rats!

Mandy pushed open the front door and led the way into the reception area, a big, square room that must have once been the entrance hall to the house. Behind the desk at the far end of the room stood Mrs. Mason, the doctor's wife. She was a tall, attractive woman with shoulder-length auburn hair, and right now she was cradling the phone between her shoulder and ear while she sifted through a heap of papers in her in-tray.

"Ah, here it is," Mandy heard her say. "The consultant at the hospital is very pleased with your progress, but you'll need to come in for one more appointment." She arranged a time for the following week and put the phone down.

"Good morning, Mrs. Mason," said Mandy, stepping forward and taking the dropper bottle out of her pocket. "We've brought the eyedrops for Jigsaw and Puzzle."

"Oh, how kind of you," said Mrs. Mason. She looked more relieved than Mandy expected for the delivery of some animal medicine. "For a minute there, I thought you'd come to make an appointment," the doctor's wife went on. She tucked a strand of hair behind one ear and glanced around the crowded waiting room. All of the chairs were taken. Despite the central heating, several of the patients were bundled up in heavy coats, looking very miserable.

"With this flu going around, we're booked solid for the next two days. I just hope we're over the worst of the epidemic by Christmas," Mrs. Mason added as the phone rang again. "Excuse me a moment," she said to Mandy and Dr. Emily. She listened to the caller while leafing through her appointment book. "The earliest I can give you is twelve-thirty on Thursday afternoon," she explained.

Mrs. Mason wrote down the patient's name in the time slot. "We'll see you then, Mrs. Davis," she said and hung up. "It's like a madhouse in here," she joked, reaching forward to take the small medicine bottle from Mandy. "I'll have to make an appointment for Jigsaw and Puzzle to see the doctor so he can put in the drops."

"Oh, we'll do that," Mandy offered as the phone rang again.

"That's very kind of you," said Mrs. Mason, her hand on the receiver. "Would you mind finding your own way upstairs?"

"Of course not," said Dr. Emily. She and Mandy went through the white-painted door marked PRIVATE at the end of the waiting room. On the other side, a flight of stairs led up to the second floor where the Masons lived.

Jigsaw and Puzzle lived in a spotlessly clean cage in the living room. The large cage stood on a table next to the window overlooking the village green. Knowing how fond Dr. Mason was of his rats, Mandy guessed he'd put the cage there so that Jigsaw and Puzzle had a view of the outside world.

"Anyone home?" she called softly, going over to the table. Inside the cage, there were two levels, with ramps leading up to a sleeping platform. There were also two exercise wheels, one on the lower level and one on the platform; a tunnel; a heap of fresh straw for burrowing into; a cozy wooden box where the rats slept; and, today, just outside the cage, a miniature imitation Christmas tree complete with tiny decorations.

Dr. Mason was obviously making sure his beloved pets didn't miss out on the holiday festivities!

"I bet there'll be some little presents around the tree on Christmas morning." Mandy chuckled.

"It wouldn't surprise me at all." Her mom smiled.

Mandy peered into the cage, tapping the wire mesh. "Jigsaw! Puzzle!"

A twitching black nose appeared just inside the wooden box.

"Come on. Out you come," Mandy said, and as if it was obeying her, a sleek black-and-white rat popped out of the box and scampered over to the wire.

"Now, which one are you?" Mandy asked, pushing her finger through the wire. The rat, which was just a bit bigger than a gerbil, sniffed at her hand. "Jigsaw or Puzzle?"

She hadn't figured out the answer yet when a second rat emerged from the nest and ran to the side of the cage as well. She was practically identical to her companion with a shiny black-and-white coat, a long black tail, and bright black eyes that were watery and red-rimmed because of the infection.

"And hello to you, too," Mandy said when the rat stood up on her hind legs and pressed her tiny front paws against the wire. The first rat quickly did the same as if she was competing for her attention.

At last, Mandy could tell the two apart because the first rat, Puzzle, had a white splash on her chest while Jigsaw's chest was mainly black with only a tiny patch of white.

"We'll treat them one at a time," said Dr. Emily, taking the dropper bottle from Mandy. "You hold them while I put in the drops."

Jigsaw scratched at the wire with her tiny claws, while Puzzle seemed content just to watch Mandy and her mom.

"OK, OK," Mandy said to Jigsaw. "I'm going to take you out now." She opened the gate in the top of the cage and reached in to close her hand around Jigsaw's tummy.

The rat's fur felt silky and soft, and she seemed to relax in Mandy's gentle hold. With her other hand, Mandy stroked the rat's back while her mom examined both eyes before putting a drop of antibiotic liquid in the corner of each one.

"You're all done," said Dr. Emily. "Now it's Puzzle's turn."

Mandy was about to return Jigsaw to the cage when the rat slipped out of her hand, ran up her arm, then sat on her shoulder and began licking her earlobe.

"Hey, that tickles!" Mandy laughed. She tried to catch Jigsaw again but the rat ran quick as a flash across her neck and sat on her other shoulder.

"You little monkey." She chuckled, at last managing to close her fingers around Jigsaw and hold her in front of her face.

The playful little creature blinked at Mandy, then brought both front paws up to her eyes and rubbed at them vigorously.

"It looks like she's crying," Mandy remarked.

"She's probably just trying to wipe away the eye-drops," said her mother.

Mandy returned Jigsaw to her cage, then took out

Puzzle, who sat quietly in her hand while Dr. Emily treated her.

"They're really the sweetest little animals," Mandy said when she put Puzzle back in the cage.

"Yes. A lot nicer than most people realize," said Dr. Emily.

"I know what you mean," Mandy said, making sure the gate was properly shut. "When I told some of my friends at school about Jigsaw and Puzzle, they were really surprised that I like them so much. They think rats are dirty, and that they can make people sick." She pushed her fingers through the wire to give Jigsaw and Puzzle a final scratch on their heads before following her mom out of the room.

"Some rats do carry disease," said Dr. Emily. "But not domestic rats that are kept clean like these."

Down in the waiting room, a small boy was just coming through the door. A girl about the same age as Mandy walked next to him, both being shepherded along by a slim, brown-haired woman who looked very troubled.

"It's Mrs. Benn," said Mandy, recognizing Sergeant Benn's family: six-year-old Harvey, his sister, Chloe, who was thirteen, and their mom, Shula. Sergeant Benn was the local police officer who lived in a house at the other end of the village from Animal Ark. Harvey was as pale as a ghost and seemed very frail. When a fit of coughing seized him, he had to stop and hug his ribs.

"It sounds like Harvey's got the flu, too," Mandy said to her mom.

"Could be," agreed Dr. Emily.

While Mrs. Benn went over to the desk to talk to the doctor's wife, Chloe helped her brother onto an empty chair. There weren't any other vacant ones nearby so she knelt down next to him. "Do you want to read a book?" she asked. "Or play a game?" She pointed to a basket of colorful toys.

Harvey shook his head and started to cough again. Chloe gently patted his back, biting her lower lip. Mandy didn't know Chloe very well because she went to a different school, but she could see she was very worried about her brother.

"Hello, Harvey," Mandy said sympathetically, crouching down in front of the little boy. "Has the flu got you, too?"

The curly-haired little boy looked at Mandy with huge green eyes but said nothing. His chest heaved as he battled to breathe.

Mandy saw that Chloe had dark rings under her eyes and that her face was drawn and pale. "You look really tired."

"I am," said Chloe, pushing a strand of auburn hair off her forehead. "We were up with Harvey all night."

The little boy started to cough again, his face turning red. Dr. Emily came to stand behind him and gently rubbed his back while Chloe looked helplessly at her mom.

The attack left Harvey looking worn out and he sat leaning forward with his shoulders hunched up and his head drooping.

"That sounds like asthma," Emily Hope said to Mrs. Benn, who had hurried over from the reception desk.

Another person had gone in to see the doctor, leaving a spare chair on the other side of the room. Mandy dragged it over and put it next to Harvey for Mrs. Benn.

"Yes, it is asthma," said Shula Benn, sitting down and giving Mandy a grateful smile. "He's had it since he was about two but he's never been this bad before." She hunted around in her handbag and brought out an inhaler.

"It sounds like he could have bronchitis as well," suggested Dr. Emily.

"That's what Dr. Mason said when we called him this morning," Mrs. Benn admitted.

Harvey looked up at his mom and Dr. Emily. "What's brotitis?" he asked in a breathless little voice.

"It's when your airways become a little sore and swollen," Dr. Emily told him, and Mandy knew her mom was keeping the explanation as simple as possible.

"Like when I sprained my ankle and it puffed up?"

"In a way." Mandy smiled and exchanged a glance with Chloe, who managed to smile, too.

Mrs. Benn tousled her son's hair. "Yes, but your ankle got better on its own," she reminded him. "If you've got bronchitis, you'll need to take some medicine to get better."

Harvey's face crumpled. "I hate medicine!" he wailed and burst into another coughing fit.

His mother wearily shook her head. "Calm down, Harvey. You know it only makes you worse when you get upset."

"But I don't want any medicine," the boy insisted.

Chloe pulled a big yellow plastic truck out of the toy basket. "Look at this!" she exclaimed brightly. "It's just like the one you've got at home."

"No it's not," said Harvey. He took the truck from her and looked at it closely. "Mine's bigger. But this one's OK, I guess." He put the toy on his lap and ran it back and forth.

Mrs. Benn smiled at Chloe. "Thanks, love."

Just then, Dr. Mason came out of his room. He had a broad, friendly face and thick silver hair. He went over to the desk and picked up a file. "Harvey Benn?" he called, reading the name on the folder. Spotting Dr. Emily and Mandy, he raised his eyebrows so that Mandy responded to his silent question.

"Jigsaw and Puzzle have had their eyedrops," she told him.

"Splendid!" said Dr. Mason, giving Mandy a thumbs-up. His blue eyes twinkled as he looked at Harvey over the top of his glasses. "Let's see if we can make this young man better, too."

Mrs. Benn and Harvey followed the doctor into the examining room. Chloe was about to go, too, but Dr. Emily suggested she stay in the waiting room. "We'll keep you company," she said.

Chloe looked surprised, then nodded. "OK," she said, sitting back down. "Who are Jigsaw and Puzzle?" she asked Mandy once the doctor's door was closed.

"Er . . . Dr. Mason's pets." Mandy hesitated. "They're rats," she finished and, exchanging a quick look with her mom, prepared herself for the usual response of *Yuck!* or *Gross!*

"Pet rats! Great!" Chloe exclaimed, her shyness giving way to enthusiasm.

"You like rats?" Mandy gasped in disbelief.

"Of course," said Chloe. "They're just as nice as other pets, aren't they?"

"*I* think so," Mandy agreed. "Do you have any pets?"

Chloe looked sad. "I wish."

"Me, too," said Mandy.

"What do you mean, you wish you had pets?" said Dr. Emily. "You're surrounded by animals every day!"

"I know," said Mandy. "It's OK, really." She'd long ago resigned herself to her parents decision that they couldn't have any pets of their own, in order to concentrate on the animals who came to the clinic.

"Do you have a lot to do with the animals at Animal Ark?" asked Chloe.

"Yup. Especially the ones that have to stay in residential care," Mandy said. "I usually feed them and clean their cages."

"That must be wonderful," said Chloe wistfully.

"Would you like to come over and meet some of the patients?" Mandy offered, thinking it might help to take Chloe's mind off her brother for a while.

Chloe's hazel eyes lit up. "I'd love to!" she exclaimed and, looking at Dr. Emily, added politely, "If I may."

"Of course," said Emily. "Why don't you come by tomorrow?"

"Great," said Mandy. "That's settled!"

"How's Harvey today?" Mandy asked Chloe when she arrived at Animal Ark the next afternoon.

"Still very sick," Chloe replied, following Mandy through the waiting room. "He's definitely got bronchitis, like your mom said. Dr. Mason gave him some yellow medicine. He really hates it, though, and it's a battle to get him to take it."

"Sounds like some animals I know," Mandy said. "They refuse to open their mouths or swallow when we give them pills. Some of them even keep the pills inside their cheeks and spit them out when we're not looking."

"Don't tell Harvey that," said Chloe. "He'll try doing the same thing."

Mandy introduced her to Jean Knox, the clinic receptionist. She was almost as busy as Mrs. Mason had been yesterday, pausing just long enough to smile at Chloe and say, "Nice to meet you, dear," before returning to the computer.

"Would you like to see the treatment rooms?" Mandy asked Chloe, who nodded eagerly.

Mandy opened a door marked EXAMINING ROOM 1 and peered inside. Dr. Adam Hope, dressed in a white coat and with a stethoscope around his neck, was trying to examine the ears of a young brindle boxer that was standing on the stainless steel table in the center of the room. Even though Simon, the veterinary nurse, was doing his best to keep the dog still, it managed to squirm and shake its head so that it was almost impossible for Dr. Adam to have a good look at it.

"That dog's even worse than Harvey." Chloe chuckled, peering over Mandy's shoulder.

At that moment, the boxer spotted them looking in at the door. He gave an excited *yip* and nearly succeeded in leaping off the table, but Dr. Adam caught his collar just in time and said firmly, "No you don't, Oberon. Not until I'm finished checking you."

"Sorry," said Mandy, catching her dad's eye. She and Chloe quickly retreated and shut the door behind them. "Let's find out who my mom's treating," Mandy said. She opened the door to the second treatment room just wide enough to see inside.

Dr. Emily had her back to them. She was dressed in a green surgical gown and was bending over the table.

"Operation, I think," Mandy said.

Hearing her, Dr. Emily looked around. Her face and nose were covered with a mask made from the same green fabric as her gown. "Hi, love. Need something?" she asked, her voice muffled by the mask.

"No. Just showing Chloe around," Mandy said. "You doing an operation?"

"Just finished actually," said Dr. Emily. She moved aside and Mandy saw an anesthetized cat, partially covered with a green cloth and lying on its side.

"I guess we'll meet her later on when she wakes up," Mandy said. She closed the door again and said to Chloe, "We'll go to the residential unit where animals stay after they've had operations."

She led Chloe into the large, airy room that had several rows of cages lining the walls. "Just three patients at the moment," said Mandy.

They went inside, being careful to close the door behind them. A plump tabby cat stared at them from the first cage with a snooty expression on his handsome face.

"Meet Mugwump," Mandy said.

Just seeing the cat seemed to help lift Chloe's mood. The tense look on her face disappeared and was replaced by a broad smile. "What a name!" She chuckled, pushing her fingers through the bars.

Mugwump looked disdainfully at Chloe's hand.

"He's very aloof," she remarked, still grinning.

"That's why his owners called him Mugwump," Mandy explained. "They said it means a big chief."

"It suits him perfectly," said Chloe. "Why's he in the hospital?"

"He had to be neutered because he was starting to wander off. His owners didn't want to be responsible for a million more Mugwumps." Mandy chuckled.

The next cage held a white hamster.

"And who are you?" asked Chloe, bending down for a closer look at the little creature whose cheek pouches were bulging with nuts.

"Would you believe she's called Ming China?" Mandy said.

Chloe laughed softly. "Makes sense for a Chinese hamster."

"Have you seen Chinese hamsters before?" Mandy asked as they moved on to a cage where a small mongrel puppy was sleeping off the anesthetic after an operation to repair a hernia.

Chloe shrugged. "No, but I'm always reading about animals," she said and looked longingly at the pup.

Mandy heard the door open behind them. She turned around. "Oh, hi, James. I thought you'd gone to Walton with your mom today to buy a new school uniform."

Eleven-year-old James Hunter was Mandy's best friend. "Luckily, a friend who Mom hasn't seen for about five years called to say she was in Welford so Mom invited her over. I stayed long enough to say hi, then said I had to take Blackie out for a walk," he explained. Blackie was James's Labrador, a gorgeous, fun-loving dog with a permanent smile on his handsome face.

"You mean, Blackie had to take *you* for a walk," Mandy teased.

James made a face as he closed the door behind him. "You know as well as I do that Blackie's totally under my control," he said, going over to Mandy and Chloe. "He's just a little boisterous, that's all."

"A little!" Mandy echoed. "That's the understatement of the year."

Then Mandy realized an introduction was in order.

"James, this is my friend Chloe," Mandy said.

"Nice to meet you," said James.

"Where's Blackie now?" asked Chloe.

"Outside, on the porch," James answered. "He was watching two blackbirds on the lawn when I left him."

They said good-bye to Mugwump and Ming China before going back into the reception room. Dr. Adam was dragging a fir tree in through the door.

"Ah!" He smiled as Mandy and her two friends came in. "Just the people I needed to do the trimming. This magnificent tree has been waiting in the garage all day to come in and make the place look festive." He heaved the tree upright and pushed the bottom into a bucket filled with damp sand. Jean Knox walked into the waiting room carrying a cardboard box full of tinsel and ornaments. "You're off the hook now, Jean." Dr. Adam chuckled. "I've recruited three volunteers for tree-trimming duty."

"Just as well," said Jean as the phone started to ring.

Dr. Adam turned to Mandy and said, "I'll leave it to you three, then," before going back into his examining room.

"Let's get started," said James. He opened the box and pulled out a long string of silver tinsel.

Chloe knelt beside him and picked up a box of small wooden reindeer. "These are cute!" She stood up and began to hang the brightly painted ornaments on the tips of the branches. Mandy crouched down to cover the bucket with a strip of red foil.

James selected a shiny green ornament and stood on a chair to hang it near the top of the tree. "What are you hoping you'll get for Christmas, Mandy?" He puffed, looking down at her through the branches.

"I saw a sweater in a shop in Walton the other day," said Mandy. "It had different breeds of dogs all over it."

"That sounds gorgeous," said Chloe. She had finished hanging up the reindeer and was trying to untangle several strands of fairy lights.

"What about you, James?" Mandy prompted. "What's on your list?"

"Some new computer software," he answered. "There's a great program that's just come out that you can use for making awesome labels and posters."

Mandy chuckled. "Typical computer geek."

"Just as long as you don't call me a nerd." James grinned.

"Geek suits you better," Mandy responded. She backed out from under the tree and smiled at Chloe. "So what about you? What are you hoping for this Christmas?"

"Nothing that can be wrapped," said Chloe. She stopped fiddling with the lights and looked down at her hands. Suddenly, she looked as tense and worried as she had in the doctor's office the day before. "The only thing I want is for Harvey to get well again."

Two

"This chocolate cake's delicious," Mandy said, helping herself to another slice that was oozing with icing and with a dusting of sugar on top to look like snow.

"Harvey helped me bake it," said Chloe. She looked across the table at her brother. "Didn't you, Harv?"

It was two days later and Mandy and James were at the Benns' house. Chloe had invited them over to celebrate Christmas early and the end of the term for both their schools.

Harvey met his sister's gaze and nodded seriously. "I stirred the mixture. And licked the bowl afterward."

"Licking the bowl is the best part about baking," put in James, loading his plate with a mince pie, two slices of chocolate cake, and a couple of meringue cookies.

"What about eating the end product?" Mandy joked, eyeing the heaped-up plate.

James shrugged. "Well, it would be a shame to waste all that hard work."

After their snack, they went to the living room, where Chloe brought out a game of Twister.

"Excellent!" exclaimed James. "I haven't played Twister since last Christmas."

"I thought you'd been put off it for life," Mandy teased. "You ended up getting squashed just about every time we played."

James pushed his glasses up on his nose. "Yeah. It got a bit rough," he admitted. "But you got flattened a few times, too, remember."

"Not as much as you did," Mandy retorted.

"Let's see if you're still the underdog, James." Chloe smiled, unfolding the white plastic mat with its brightly colored circles.

Harvey had flopped onto the sofa in front of the TV but now he slid down and sat cross-legged on the floor next to the mat. "I want to play, too," he said.

Chloe looked doubtfully at him. "Are you sure?"

"Yes," came the eager reply.

"But Twister can get a little wild, remember, and Dr. Mason said you had to rest," she reminded him.

"I rested this morning," Harvey insisted.

Chloe shrugged. "OK." Harvey took the spinner out of the Twister box.

Then he broke into a coughing fit.

Chloe was at his side in a flash. "Are you OK?"

Harvey couldn't reply and they all watched helplessly until the attack subsided. At last, Harvey stopped coughing and sat wheezing loudly, his breath coming in short, shallow puffs.

Mandy exchanged a worried glance with James. "Are you absolutely sure you want to play this rough game?" she asked the little boy.

Harvey's shoulders heaved. "Yes," he said. "I'm fine."

"You know what I think," said Chloe immediately. "We should go in order of age. Oldest one first. So that's me." She quickly spun the dial to find out which circle she had to put her hand on. "Red," she said when the dial stopped.

Mandy's turn was next, then James, and finally Harvey. It wasn't long before they were all in a complete tangle, with Mandy arched high over the mat, James underneath, Chloe bunched up tightly next to him, and Harvey almost submerged by them all.

"It feels like I've gotten stuck doing push-ups." James puffed.

"Better than having to balance on the tips of your fingers and toes." Mandy laughed.

"You OK, Harv?" Chloe asked.

"Your elbow's in my face," he complained, his voice muffled. "And I can't breathe right because James is squashing me."

"Sorry," said Chloe and she moved her arm while James tried to wriggle away from Harvey.

Mandy felt James bump against her foot. "Careful." She gasped.

"Too bad," teased James.

"You're still poking me in the face, Chloe," whined Harvey and he collapsed in a heap. "That's not fair!" he wailed, rolling off the mat. "You were poking me in my face."

"All right, all right," said Chloe patiently. "You can take my place." She began to wriggle from beneath the other two but Harvey stood up and said, "I don't want to play this game anymore. It's stupid."

"Well, what *do* you want to play?" asked Chloe just as James crashed to the ground, bumping heavily into Mandy's legs so that she fell flat on her face as well.

"How about that!" exclaimed Chloe, standing up. "I'm the winner." She smiled encouragingly at Harvey, who had climbed onto the couch and was sitting in one corner with his legs drawn up against his chest. "Why don't you choose another game for us all to play?"

Harvey hugged his knees. "I don't want to play anything," he said angrily, coughing.

"What about Toppling Tower?" Mandy asked, seeing a tall box of wooden bricks on a bookshelf.

"I hate Toppling Tower," grumbled Harvey. "The stupid thing always falls down." He looked out the window at the sleety rain. "I wish we were at Euro Disney."

"You know we're going there in the spring," said Chloe with a sigh. She started to pack away the Twister mat and added quietly to Mandy, "We were supposed to go to Euro Disney in Paris last weekend but Mom and Dad had to cancel it because of Harvey being sick."

"That's too bad," said Mandy. "But maybe it'll be better in the spring when it's warmer."

"I wanted to go *now*!" Harvey wailed, overhearing them. "It's boring at home." He picked up the remote and switched on the TV. A game of soccer filled the screen.

"Cool!" said James, who was crazy about soccer. He sat down next to Harvey but the little boy immediately flicked over to another program, this time a soap opera.

Harvey flicked through the rest of the channels, then switched off the set. "I don't want to watch TV. I want to play Chutes and Ladders." He yawned and rubbed his eyes.

"Maybe you should take a nap," suggested Chloe.

"I'm not tired," Harvey insisted.

Mandy glanced at her watch. "Er, I think we ought to go," she said, shooting James a meaningful look.

"Yeah," James said, understanding at once. "I've got homework to do."

Chloe looked surprised. "But school's finished."

"It's, er, a project," said James and before he had to go into any more detail, the door opened and Sergeant Benn came in. He was wearing his policeman's uniform and Mandy guessed he'd just come off duty.

"Sorry to crash the party," he said cheerfully, taking off his helmet and putting it on the coffee table. He ran one hand through his thick black hair so that it stood on end.

"You're not crashing. It was over," Chloe told her dad.

"Yes, Harvey's a bit worn out. We thought we'd better go so he can get some rest," Mandy explained.

Sergeant Benn looked at his son. "Mmm. Still not feeling too good, eh? Well, let's see what we can do about that."

Without another word, he went out of the living room and came back carrying two big boxes wrapped in Christmas wrapping paper. There was a bunch of roses lying on the top box. "Shula!" he called over his shoulder. "Are you coming to see what I've brought home?"

"Be there in a sec," called Mrs. Benn.

The sight of the presents perked Harvey up at once. "Are they for me?" he asked, slipping off the couch and going over to his father.

"One is. And the other's for Chloe," said Sergeant Benn, his brown eyes twinkling.

Mrs. Benn came in, folding a pair of jeans. "It looks like Christmas has come early," she remarked. She frowned at her husband as he handed her the roses. "What's all this about?"

Sergeant Benn put the boxes side by side on the coffee table. The larger one, which had a bright red ribbon tied around it, was close to the edge. Mandy thought she heard a dull thud from inside, and the whole box twitched. It nearly fell to the floor but Chloe's dad caught it and pushed it to the center of the table. "Seeing as we had to cancel our weekend in Paris, I thought you all deserved a treat," he said.

Mrs. Benn hugged him. "You're a big softy."

"I don't think the fellow I ticketed this morning for leaving his car in a no-parking zone would say so," said the sergeant with a laugh. He pointed to the smaller present and said to Harvey, "That's yours, son. Open it up."

Harvey picked up the box, then sat cross-legged on

the carpet and started tearing at the wrapping paper. A short spell of coughing interrupted him and Mandy saw Chloe bite her lip, but Harvey recovered and pulled off the last of the paper. "Cool! It's a toy garage!" he exclaimed. Flushed with excitement, he pulled out all the pieces. There were gas pumps complete with little plastic hoses, a tiny shop, several cars, and even a miniature car wash.

"Thanks, Dad!" said the little boy, and he immediately lay on his tummy amid the torn wrapping paper and started assembling the garage.

Mrs. Benn smiled at her husband. "Good choice," she said approvingly.

"I hope you think the same about Chloe's gift," remarked Sergeant Benn. "Careful how you handle it, love. It's fragile."

Looking at the box, Mandy noticed a few small holes in the top. *Air holes?* she wondered and glanced at Sergeant Benn.

But Sergeant Benn wasn't giving anything away and Mandy was left in the dark.

"Maybe it's a computer?" James suggested as Chloe picked up the box and sat on the sofa with it on her lap.

Chloe shot him a glance that seemed to say she hoped it wasn't. She untied the ribbon then peeled off the tape and unwrapped the paper, folding it up neatly. Inside was a green-and-red cardboard box marked GRANNY SMITH APPLES.

"Great! You can make apple pies for everyone," James joked.

"Oh sure." Chloe chuckled.

Mandy was certain that the box would contain something a lot more exciting than fruit. But in her wildest dreams she'd never have guessed what it was. Because when Chloe finally took off the lid, out burst a gorgeous golden-coated puppy!

Three

"I can't believe it!" Chloe laughed, cuddling the cocker spaniel puppy who wriggled in her arms and looked just as excited as her new owner.

"She's absolutely adorable," Mandy agreed, smoothing the silky dog while James crouched down next to them and held out his hand for the puppy to sniff.

The little dog looked up at him, with her tail wagging at top speed and her tongue hanging out in a wide canine grin.

Sergeant Benn watched with his arms folded and a broad smile on his face. "I knew you'd like her," he said to Chloe.

31

"She's the best present in the world." Chloe smiled.
"Thank you, Dad. Handing the puppy to Mandy, she
jumped up to give her dad a big hug.

Mrs. Benn seemed a lot less enthusiastic. "I'm not
sure this is the right time for us to have a pet," she said,
glancing down at Harvey, who was still stretched out on
the floor, playing with his garage.

He'd lined up the cars next to the gas pumps and
was pretending to fill their fuel tanks. "Glug, glug, glug,"
he said, holding the miniature hose against one of the
cars.

"Oh, it'll be fine," said Sergeant Benn. "Chloe de-
serves the pup. She's proved how responsible she is
with the way she's helped to look after Harvey."

But Mandy found herself sharing Mrs. Benn's feel-
ings. A puppy needed a lot of attention, but with Harvey
not being well, there could be times when this one
would end up being overlooked. And what troubled
Mandy even more was that the tiny spaniel was a
Christmas gift. She believed very strongly in the saying
that pets were for life, not just for Christmas.

*But, like Sergeant Benn said, Chloe's very responsi-
ble. Caring, too,* Mandy argued with herself. She caught
James's eye and he raised his eyebrows so that Mandy
knew he was having similar thoughts. The two friends
had come across enough unwanted and abandoned

pets that had started out as Christmas presents with the best intentions.

"Where did you get her?" Chloe asked her dad, taking the puppy back from Mandy and rubbing her face against its velvety head.

"From an animal sanctuary near York," said Sergeant Benn. "Her mother was taken there by some people who found her wandering along the main road. The woman who runs the sanctuary thinks she was dumped because she was pregnant."

Another unlucky Christmas present? Mandy couldn't help wondering.

"Apparently, she was in bad shape," Sergeant Benn went on. "So it was really something when she gave birth to three healthy pups. They've all been checked and given their shots by the local vet. When I heard they were looking for a home, I knew of the ideal place for one of them." He put his arm around Chloe's shoulders.

"And to think I'd given up on having a pet of my own until I left home," murmured Chloe, kissing the squirming puppy on top of her head.

"Well, now that you have one, you'd better keep in mind that it's your puppy, not mine," said Mrs. Benn. "And that means feeding her, cleaning up after her, taking her out for a walk before you go to school and again when you come home, brushing her. . . ."

"I know, I know." Chloe sighed, sounding impatient.

"Training her, too," Mandy couldn't resist adding. She knew that well-behaved dogs stood a much better chance of having a permanent home than dogs who'd had no guidance from their owners and so ended up being a nuisance.

"I'll do all those things," Chloe reassured everyone. "Starting right now. I'm going to teach her to sit." She put the puppy on the floor and knelt down in front of her.

Mandy watched Chloe gently pushing the pup's rump. "Sit," Chloe said.

But the little dog had other plans. She shook herself vigorously, then bounded over to Harvey.

Chloe crawled after her but the puppy hurtled into the toy garage, sending the cars flying and knocking over the car wash and pumps.

"Hey! Get off," yelled Harvey as the puppy rolled on top of the tiny shop before picking up one of the gas pumps and running off with it in her mouth. "That's mine. Give it back!" Turning to his mom, he wailed, "Look what it's done! It's a horrible dog." He got up to chase after the puppy but started coughing so much that he had to stop.

Mrs. Benn looked furious. "I knew this kind of thing

would happen," she said, storming over to Harvey and rubbing his back.

"It's just an accident," Sergeant Benn said calmly. "I'll get Harvey's inhaler." He hurried out of the room.

Mandy felt embarrassed and when she glanced at James, she saw that he looked uncomfortable, too.

Meanwhile, Chloe was trying to get the gas pump away from the puppy. But the spaniel dived under a chair with the toy still firmly wedged between her teeth.

"She's going to break it," Harvey sobbed, and he

dropped onto his knees to crawl under the chair where the puppy was hiding.

With an excited yelp, the puppy shot past Harvey and scampered under another chair where she lay with her chin on her front paws, gazing mischievously out at everyone.

Normally, Mandy would have found her playfulness amusing, but with Harvey getting more worked up by the second and Mrs. Benn looking very annoyed, the situation wasn't in the least funny. She looked for something to distract the puppy and her eyes fell on the ribbon that had been tied around the box. She picked it up and gave it to Chloe. "Try dragging this across the floor," she suggested. "She might want to chase after it."

"Good idea," said Chloe. She wiggled the ribbon in front of the chair, then pulled it slowly away.

The trick worked. The spaniel instantly let go of the toy and scurried after the ribbon, trying to stop it with her front paws, then scampering after it again when she couldn't.

Harvey grabbed the gas pump and, still wheezing, returned sulkily to his game just as his dad came in with the inhaler and helped him to take a puff of the medicine. James went over to help Harvey set up the garage again. He collected the cars that had spun all over the floor and started lining them up.

Chloe shot Mandy a grateful look. "Thanks," she said and let go of the ribbon so that the puppy caught it in her mouth. She shook it so vigorously that she toppled over, wrapping the ribbon around her plump little tummy.

This time, Mandy couldn't help laughing. "You look like a trussed chicken," she said. "And you look as if you've just eaten a whole chicken, too," she added, noticing how round the little dog's belly was.

"She does have a fat tummy," agreed Chloe.

To Mandy's eyes, though, it was more than just fat. It seemed rather bloated. But at the same time, Mandy could feel her ribs sticking out beneath her golden coat.

"You'd better take that dog outside," Mrs. Benn told Chloe. "Next thing she'll be messing indoors and then I *will* blow a fuse."

Chloe scooped up the puppy. "Coming, Mandy?"

They grabbed their coats from the hall and went out into the backyard. Chloe put the puppy on the lawn and the little dog began sniffing around, not bothered by the drizzle that was falling.

"She's really confident and even though she's a bit of a toy thief, she has a lovely temperament," Mandy remarked.

"She does," Chloe agreed proudly.

The puppy was sniffing around next to the wooden fence. She squatted down to relieve herself.

"Good girl," Chloe called to her. "Now we can get out of this rain."

The puppy seemed to be taking her time and Mandy noticed that she had a bit of an upset tummy. She was about to say something but changed her mind. Puppies often had upset tummies, and it might explain the swollen belly.

"Come on," Chloe called to the pup. She crouched down and clapped her hands together. "We're getting drenched out here."

The little spaniel looked at her new owner then stood up and bounded over to her with her mouth open and her pink tongue hanging out so that she looked as if she was laughing. She leaped into Chloe's outstretched arms and snuggled up against her. With her head resting on Chloe's hand, she gazed at Mandy with dark, trusting eyes. It was as if she was saying, *This is where I belong.*

"She definitely thinks you're the right owner for her." Mandy smiled as they turned to go back into the house. "What are you going to name her?"

"I've been thinking about that," said Chloe. "She reminds me of a book I read. A girl and her mother lost their home during a war. They had nowhere to go and had to sleep out in the open, and they had to do all sorts of things like washing and window cleaning just to get enough money for food."

"How does that remind you of this puppy?" Mandy asked, opening the kitchen door.

"Well, the girl had golden hair, too, and in the end she and her mother made friends with some people who found them a great home, just like I'm going to give . . ." She paused and, looking at the puppy, said, "Indy. Which is what the girl in the story was called."

"I like that," said Mandy. But in her heart, she really hoped that this story would have a happy ending, too, and Indy wouldn't find herself looking for a new home once the novelty of having her had worn off.

Four

"Look! There's Chloe and Indy," Mandy told her gran and James as they came around the corner on their way to the post office.

It was Saturday morning, with just over a week to go before Christmas. Mandy and James were helping Gran to mail her Christmas cards. But even more important, they were on a mission to find people to donate prizes for the raffle that was to be held at the Christmas fair in five days. Although Gran had been looking for prizes for a couple of weeks, she'd only had two offers so far: Lydia Fawcett from High Cross farm had donated a month's supply of goat's milk, while the owner of a fleet of rowing boats moored upstream from Welford had offered the loan of a boat for an afternoon.

"Not a lot of people are interested in winning either of those," Gran had confessed to Mandy and James that morning when the three of them and Blackie had set out from Lilac Cottage where Gran and Grandpa Hope lived. "Goat's milk is a bit of an acquired taste, and a boat ride in winter isn't exactly appealing. We've hardly sold any tickets, and we were hoping to raise a lot of money for the children's ward at the Cottage Hospital this year."

"Don't worry, Mandy and I will persuade lots of people to give prizes," James had promised. Laughing, he'd rolled his hands into fists and flexed his arm muscles.

"That should do it," Mandy had said with a chuckle. "And Blackie will definitely make a difference. People will offer anything to make sure you don't let him jump up on them."

"He's not that bad," James had responded, looking a little hurt.

As James had said, the glossy black Labrador wasn't that bad at all. In fact, he'd been as good as gold so far this morning. The only person he'd jumped on was James when he'd bent down to tie his shoelace.

But the spell of good behavior was short-lived. The instant Blackie caught sight of Indy outside the post office with Chloe, he charged forward with his ears pricked up.

Caught off guard, James was almost pulled off his feet. "Heel, Blackie!" he ordered. But he might as well have said *Full steam ahead* because Blackie just pulled harder.

"What did you say the other day about Blackie being under your control?" Mandy teased, walking fast to keep up with them.

Unable to match their pace, Gran fell behind.

"He *is* under control most of the time," James insisted breathlessly. "It's just that he's never seen Indy before."

"Oh, sure." Mandy chuckled. "And what about ducks and cats and other dogs he knows and . . . "

"All right, all right," James said testily. "I can't help it if he's curious."

Chloe looked alarmed as Blackie surged toward her and the puppy. She bent down to pick Indy up and held her protectively against her coat.

"It's OK." James puffed as they reached her and skidded to a halt. "He won't hurt Indy."

Chloe didn't look convinced, especially when Blackie stretched up his neck, sniffing energetically. His head dwarfed the little dog, who tried to shrink away. Chloe lifted her up to her shoulder where the puppy nuzzled against her neck.

"James is right," Mandy reassured her. "He's just a big friendly boy." She patted Blackie's head, then closed her hand around his collar and gently pulled him away.

"Sit, Blackie," James ordered and, to Chloe's obvious relief, the boisterous Labrador obeyed.

James looked a little surprised, but he quickly took out a dog biscuit and gave it to Blackie, then offered one to the puppy.

Indy looked at the biscuit but she didn't seem very interested, and didn't even bother to sniff at it.

"She's a little fussy about her food," Chloe said, and added proudly, "but she can sit now. Look." She put Indy on the ground and gave her the command.

The puppy shot Blackie a nervous glance, then pressed up against Chloe's legs and looked beseechingly at her.

"She wants to be picked up again." Mandy chuckled.

Chloe bent down and scooped her up again. "She really *does* sit when I tell her," she insisted, smoothing Indy's long, silky ears. "She's nothing like as naughty as she was that first day."

That's unusual, Mandy thought. In her experience, puppies became more of a handful as they grew older and stronger. She couldn't remember hearing about a puppy calming down so soon after it arrived at its new home. "You must have a magic touch," she said to Chloe and felt bad for the misgivings she'd had the other day about Sergeant Benn's present. It wasn't fair to think that just because Indy was a Christmas gift and had come when the Benns were having a tough time, she would end up being neglected.

Mandy ran her hand over the puppy's coat and noticed she was still bony and that her belly was just as swollen as before. But it was still early. Puppies didn't change shape overnight.

Grandma Hope caught up with them and her expression softened when she saw Indy. "Oh, my, what a beautiful dog," she said and put her hand out for Indy to sniff.

Indy just stared soulfully at her.

"A little bored with all this fussing, are we?" Gran chuckled.

"She isn't usually," Chloe said quickly. "I think she's tired. Everyone we've bumped into has wanted to say hello."

"Well, then, no wonder she's gone so quiet. She's fed up with people." Gran smiled. "Look at that expression on her sweet little face."

Indy peered at Gran through half-closed eyes.

"Mind you," Gran went on, "you're looking a little down yourself, Chloe. Is everything all right?"

"Not really," said Chloe, her face falling. She scuffed at the ground with the toe of her shoe. "Harvey had to go into the hospital."

"But I thought he was getting better," Mandy said, surprised.

Chloe shook her head. "No, he's got pneumonia now."

"That's serious!" exclaimed James, his eyes wide behind his glasses. "It's not because he got so tired the other day, is it?" Beside him, Blackie squirmed restlessly, his gaze fixed on the puppy who was now asleep in Chloe's arms.

Mandy had jumped to the same conclusion as James, but Chloe quickly reassured them. "He probably shouldn't have gotten upset, but Dr. Mason said that wouldn't have caused the pneumonia. It's an infection, just like the bronchitis was." Although she spoke with a matter-of-fact tone, a shadow crossed her face and Mandy realized that she was more worried than she was letting on.

Gran shook her head sympathetically. "Pneumonia on top of bronchitis. The poor dear."

"And he's asthmatic," said Chloe, then added stoutly, "but he'll be OK. And thanks to Indy, things aren't totally sad. She's a real clown sometimes and really cheers us up."

"Even your mom?" Mandy said disbelievingly, then wished she hadn't when the post office door opened and Mrs. Benn came out.

Luckily, Chloe's mom hadn't heard. She came down the stairs and greeted everyone. "Nearly ready for Christmas?" she asked Gran.

"Getting there," came the reply. "And you?"

"Oh, I don't know," said Mrs. Benn, and Mandy noticed that she had dark rings under her eyes and a tense look on her face. "I'm not sure we'll even get to have

Christmas this year, the way things are turning out."
She put an arm around Chloe's shoulders. "I suppose
you've heard that Harvey's in the hospital?"

"Yes, Chloe just told us," said Gran. "It must be very
difficult for you right now."

"Yes, it is," Mrs. Benn agreed. "Especially with my
husband having to work extra shifts while half the station's on vacation for the holidays. Still, I can't com-
plain," she said, trying to sound brighter. "Chloe's being
an absolute angel. I don't know how I'd manage without
her."

Chloe seemed a bit embarrassed by her mom's
praise. She looked down at Indy and wiped an invisible
speck of dirt off one of her silky ears.

"If there's anything I can do to help, just let me
know," said Grandma Hope.

"We can help out, too," Mandy offered. "Can't we,
James?"

"Um, sure," James said hesitantly. Mandy could tell,
though, that he didn't really know what they could do.
"I guess we could, er, wash windows or something," he
added.

Shula Benn smiled at them. "That's very kind of you,
but I expect we'll cope."

Gran looked thoughtful. "That's what people always

say and then, when they can't manage, they don't take up the offers of help. So I'm going to make sure that I *do* make myself useful. For starters, Chloe and the pup can come to Lilac Cottage when you visit Harvey in the hospital."

"Now that *would* be a help," Mrs. Benn said gratefully. "I don't like leaving Chloe on her own but someone has to stay behind to look after Indy."

"There you are then." Gran smiled at Chloe. "Why don't you come around tomorrow afternoon, dear?" She must have noticed Chloe looking reluctant because she quickly said, "You won't be bored, I promise. Mandy and James are coming over to help me get ready for the fair."

"Even Blackie will be there, making sure the mince pies are up to standard!" Mandy added with a grin.

Chloe looked as if she was quite eager to join in, but at the mention of Blackie her expression changed. "Blackie?" she said doubtfully and glanced at Indy. "I don't know. He might hurt Indy." Clearly, Mandy and James's earlier reassurances hadn't convinced her.

"Never!" James said at once. "Blackie might be a little energetic but he's not nasty. He'll be really gentle with her."

"And it'll be nice for Indy to have some dog company," Mandy said.

"You could use some company, too," Mrs. Benn told Chloe. "And not just dog company," she added with a smile.

After agreeing that Chloe would go to Lilac Cottage at two-thirty the next day, Mandy, James, and Gran went into the post office, leaving Blackie tied to the railing outside. That was because dogs, even those as tiny as Indy, were not allowed inside.

"Good morning, Mrs. McFarlane," said Mandy, opening the door. The jangling bell also announced their arrival.

The postmistress was standing behind the counter, stamping mail. She looked up at them. "Goodness! What a delegation! Have you come to make me buy a raffle ticket?" she joked, patting her graying hair that was drawn up in a bun on top of her head.

"No. More than that." James grinned. "We've come to persuade you to donate a prize."

"And then to buy a few tickets so you can win it back," added Gran, winking at Mandy.

"Now that's what I call a bargain." Mrs. McFarlane laughed. She put one hand in the pocket of her blue gingham overall while cupping her chin with the other and studying the shelves. "Let me see," she said, more to herself than to the others. "What would be a nice prize?" She glanced at the racks on the other side of the shop. "Something good to eat, I think," she decided out loud.

James had spotted boxes of chocolates standing upright on one shelf. "How about one of those?" he suggested.

His technique worked. The postmistress glanced at him and then at the chocolates and, without even hesitating, she reached up and took a box off the shelf. "These OK?" She smiled at Gran.

"Oh, I'd say so," answered Gran, looking very pleased. The box was too big for her basket, so Mandy took it. "That should encourage people to buy tickets."

"I'll buy dozens," James said at once, not taking his eyes off the box that Mandy held in both hands like a tray.

"I bet you wouldn't have bought any tickets if the only prize was the goat's milk," Mandy teased him.

"What do you mean?" responded James, folding his arms and managing to tear his eyes from the chocolates to look at Mandy. "Of course I'd have bought some. It's all for a good cause, you know."

They thanked Mrs. McFarlane and promised to come back soon with a raffle sheet so she could buy some tickets. Outside, James untied Blackie, then, with the dog walking calmly to heel, they went to the Fox and Goose restaurant.

The owner, Julian Hardy, was coming out of the low stone building carrying a string of chunky outdoor Christmas lights. "Are you looking for John?" he called.

His eleven-year-old son, John, went to boarding school in the Lake District.

"No. You're the one we need to speak to," answered Gran.

"Really? What have I done?" He grinned, pretending to look worried.

"It's what you're going to do," James put in. "We're looking for prizes for the raffle."

Julian raised his eyebrows. "So you want me to donate a year's supply of soda?"

"Maybe not soda," said Gran, looking a little anxious, which Mandy thought might have something to do with James planning on buying so many tickets. "Isn't there something else you could give? We're very short of prizes so pretty much anything is welcome."

"Even goat's milk." James grinned.

Mandy held up the giant box of chocolates. "This is what Mrs. McFarlane gave us."

"Mmm, I don't know," said Julian with a frown. He ran his hand over his curly hair. "I mean, we don't have much other than drinks to offer. Unless . . ." He glanced back at the restaurant at the side of the building. "Unless we give away a meal for two people."

"That's a grand idea," said Gran enthusiastically.

"I bet my dad would like to win that," Mandy said. "I'll buy him a few tickets as a surprise." Adam Hope enjoyed his food and he particularly liked eating at this restaurant because it was once a forge that had been owned by his grandfather many years before.

With another generous prize guaranteed, Mandy, James, and Gran felt very satisfied. They headed back to Lilac Cottage, crossing the village green where the traditional Christmas tree stood, its branches decorated with silver tinsel and hundreds of sparkling lights.

Mandy felt a shiver of excitement. Nearly everyone in Welford had strung up lights outside their homes and shops so that after dark, the village glittered like a treasure chest. "This is definitely the best place to be at Christmas," she remarked, her festive spirit going up another gear.

She caught sight of Sergeant Benn cycling down a path leading from the green. His head was down as he pedaled into the cold wind that funneled down the road. Mandy thought of Harvey lying in the hospital and she remembered what Mrs. Benn had said outside the post office: *"I'm not sure we'll get to have Christmas this year."*

"Imagine not having Christmas!" Mandy remarked out loud so that James and Gran looked at her in surprise.

"It's so unfair!" she went on. "Harvey *has* to get better soon!"

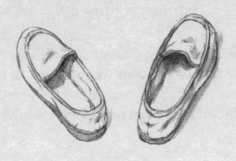

Five

"If you sit with Indy on your lap, Blackie can get to know her better," Mandy suggested to Chloe when she and the puppy arrived at Lilac Cottage the following afternoon. "Once they've had a good sniff at each other, they'll be fine."

Chloe still wasn't sure. "He's awfully big," she said as Blackie bounced around her, his tail wagging at a dizzying speed and his eyes glued on the little golden bundle in her arms.

James seemed tired of defending his dog. "Look, if you're really frightened that he'll squash her or something, I'll put him out on the front porch."

To Mandy's surprise, Chloe looked dismayed. "You can't do that. It wouldn't be fair," she said and promptly sat down on one of the kitchen chairs with Indy in her lap. "After all, this house belongs more to him than to Indy."

"It belongs to neither of them," Gran said sternly, although her eyes were twinkling.

Delighted to find himself at the puppy's level at last, Blackie sniffed Indy all over.

"He's like an oversized vacuum cleaner," Chloe said,

visibly relaxing when it became clear that Blackie didn't regard the puppy as a free meal.

Gran was transferring a batch of freshly baked mince pies from a cooling rack into a tin. She looked at Chloe and chuckled. "That's the best description I've heard of Blackie yet. He's even better than my Hoover at picking up food." As she spoke, she accidentally knocked a mince pie onto the floor.

Blackie's reaction was lightning quick. He pounced on the broken pie and devoured it in one gulp, not even bothering, as most dogs would, to sniff it to find out what it was.

"Enjoy that?" Gran laughed as Blackie looked up at her, licking his lips.

Mandy grinned. "He's waiting for you to do that again."

"No chance of that," said Gran as she carefully packed away the last few pies. "These are for the raffle." She snapped the lid shut and put the tin on a high shelf, well out of Blackie's reach.

"Pity about that," murmured James, tracking the tin and its delectable contents with his eyes.

"Like owner, like dog," Gran laughed. "But you don't need to worry, James. I have a special snack ready for us all."

James's face lit up. "Really?"

"Yes. After you've made more raffle sheets for me. I think we'll be able to get more people to buy tickets with all the new prizes we have now." Gran opened a drawer and took out a sketchpad, a collection of pens, and a couple of rulers. "I think this is all you'll need," she said.

James sat down at the table and tore some pages out of the pad. "Raffle sheets coming up," he said.

"We should make posters, too, so that people know what the raffle's for," Mandy said.

Chloe put Indy down on the floor. "What *is* it for?" she asked, glancing up at Mandy.

"The children's wing at Walton Cottage Hospital," Mandy told her.

"The same one Harvey's in?"

Gran nodded. "We're hoping to freshen the place up a bit this year with some new curtains and matching sheets. We'd also like to get some new toys for the children."

"That'll be great," said Chloe. "Some of the toys there look as if they were around in Queen Victoria's time."

"They probably were," agreed Gran, taking another tray of pies out of the oven before sliding in a batch of shortbread.

Indy was sniffing around Chloe's feet, her long, feathery tail held out behind her. "Good girl," Chloe said, evidently quite pleased that Indy didn't want to leave her side.

Mandy couldn't help thinking that the puppy should be more adventurous. It wouldn't do Indy any good to be babied. *Still, better for her to be pampered than neglected,* she told herself, unable to shake off her reservations about Indy being a Christmas present.

Blackie was sitting beside the kitchen table and staring hard at the tray of mince pies as if he was willing one to drop on the ground again. But when he realized Indy was on the floor, he gave up his food vigil and switched his attention to her.

"Gently," James warned his dog, but Blackie just lay flat on the floor and nuzzled Indy like a doting father.

"You *are* a sweet boy," Chloe smiled. "I shouldn't have worried about you for a moment."

Unlike Blackie, Indy didn't seem the least bit interested in making a new friend. She tried to back away from him, and when that didn't work and Blackie still nudged her with his wet black nose, she squeezed between Chloe's feet, looking very sorry for herself.

She's incredibly shy, Mandy thought. *That's not a very good sign.* She'd expected Indy to leap all over the big dog and entice him into a game of tag or rough-and-tumble. But perhaps the puppy just needed a little time to settle down. Mandy crouched down in front of Indy and stroked her head. "Don't you want to play with Blackie?" she said.

The Labrador was still doing his best to encourage Indy to play with him. He wriggled backward and barked softly at her.

"He's begging her to play a game," said James with a laugh.

Blackie barked again. *Come on, let's play*, he seemed to be saying. But his invitation was flatly turned down. Indy blinked at him, then made her intentions quite clear by curling up between Chloe's feet and closing her eyes.

"That's what I call giving someone the cold shoulder," remarked Gran.

"I think she's just tired," Chloe explained. "She likes to sleep a lot."

"Perhaps she's a bit overwhelmed at finding herself in a new place with a big dog bouncing around her," Gran suggested. "And her way of coping is to bury her head in the sand."

"More like between Chloe's feet," put in James.

Spurned by the tiny dog, Blackie gave up and went back to his mince-pie-watching position next to the table. Mandy felt sorry for him and slipped him a few crumbs that had collected under the cooling rack. "Maybe Indy will feel a little livelier next time," she said to the Labrador. She knew puppies needed a lot of sleep, but she still felt puzzled by Indy's behavior. The spaniel wasn't nearly as lively as when she first popped out of the apple box.

Gran opened the oven to check on the shortbread. A wave of scented heat wafted out and Mandy wondered if this could be the explanation for Indy's behavior. It was very warm and cozy in the kitchen with the oven churning out mince pies and other Christmas goodies. "You know, she's probably sleepy because it's so warm in here," Mandy said out loud.

"Could be," agreed Chloe. "She loves curling up next to the radiator at home." She picked up a raffle sheet that James had just finished making and studied it for a moment, and then, taking a blank sheet of paper, began to make another one.

"I'll start the posters," said Mandy, reaching for the markers.

When it was time for a break, Gran opened the window and called out to Grandpa who'd been puttering around in his greenhouse for most of the afternoon. "Tea's ready, Tom."

She had barely closed the window when Mandy heard her grandpa stamping mud off his boots outside the back door. Moments later, he came in with just his socks on and rubbing his hands together to warm them up. "Weather's turning colder," he remarked, pushing his feet into the old felt slippers that were behind the door. He looked at Indy curled up between Chloe's feet. "Still asleep, eh?" He'd popped in once during the afternoon to fetch some green twine and had met Chloe and her pup then.

He washed his hands at the sink, then sat down at the table and admired the completed raffle sheets and posters. "You three have been busy," he said.

"It was a real factory in here this afternoon." Gran smiled, putting a big oval plate laden with cakes, cookies, and mince pies in the middle of the table.

"If I'd had my new computer software, I could have done everything in about ten minutes flat," said James.

"Computer software? To make a few raffle sheets and posters?" said Grandpa, leaning back in his chair and shaking his head. "That just shows what this world is coming to, when we need expensive machines instead of a few pens and pencils."

"But computers make things so much easier," Mandy said, picking up the teapot that Gran had filled to pour out a cup each for her grandparents.

"And they make things look really neat," put in Chloe. At her feet, Indy rolled over and stretched. For a moment, Mandy thought she was about to wake up, but the puppy was just changing position and went straight back to sleep.

"Easier? Neat? Nonsense," argued Grandpa. "From what I've heard, computers cause all sorts of problems. Like these newfangled virus things."

"Those are created by really sick hackers," James quickly pointed out.

"If they've got viruses then they are most certainly sick," Grandpa teased.

James couldn't have noticed that Grandpa Hope was having fun with him because he pushed his glasses up on his nose and went on in a serious tone, "Most of the time, if you know how to work a computer, you shouldn't have any trouble with it."

"Well, I wouldn't know about that," said Grandpa, taking a sip of tea. "But what I can tell you is that when we were your age, we relied on ordinary pens and pencils and our own intelligence. And nothing went wrong with that." He glanced at Gran for confirmation.

"Let it drop, Tom." She chuckled.

But Grandpa was only just warming to the subject. He put his cup back in its saucer and leaned forward with his arms crossed. "The only viruses that affected us were ones that gave us the flu, not ones that made you lose all your hard work." He must have seen James roll his eyes, because he winked at Mandy and said, "Mark my words, Master Hunter, soon machines will be thinking for humans and where will we be then? People will forget how to write and count altogether!" He smoothed his gray mustache and helped himself to a piece of cake.

James gave Mandy a helpless look. "All I said was that a software package could have sped things up for us."

"Oh, don't mind him," said Gran. She pushed the plate of cookies toward James. "He's just jealous because he can't work a computer. And to tell the truth, he's probably embarrassed because you're six times younger than him and are already an expert."

Grandpa pretended to look offended. "You're all ganging up on me! Let me tell you that if I had a mind to, I could easily learn how to use a computer."

"That I'd love to see." Gran laughed.

Chloe's mom arrived to pick her up just as they were finishing their snack. Gran invited her in but Mrs. Benn said she couldn't stop as she had a lot to do at home.

On the way out to the car, Mrs. Benn glanced at the sleeping pup in Chloe's arms. "I hope Indy hasn't been any trouble," she said.

"She was a little angel," Gran told Mrs. Benn. "We hardly knew she was here."

"Yes, she must be the most well-behaved dog I've

ever seen," said Grandpa. He glanced at Blackie, who'd shot out of the door and was bounding across the front lawn toward a crow sitting on the fence. "Unlike some dogs I know."

Mandy thought that James looked offended so she quickly said, "Grandpa's only teasing you. Again."

"I know." James grinned. "But I have to admit that Indy does put Blackie to shame."

"Oh, Blackie's super," said Chloe quickly, giving the Labrador an admiring look. "But Indy *is* good. Which is probably just as well, with the way things are in our house at the moment."

"Probably," Mandy agreed. At the same time, though, she couldn't help thinking that Indy seemed too quiet. Something wasn't quite right, but she couldn't put her finger on it.

After Chloe and Mrs. Benn had driven away, Mandy and James helped to wash up before putting the posters inside a couple of plastic bags to make sure they didn't get wet or crumpled on the way home.

"We'll pin them up around the village tomorrow morning," Mandy promised.

"Thanks, dear," said Gran. "I just wish we had a few more prizes to offer."

"But what we've got is OK," Mandy reasoned. "Goat's

milk, boat ride, chocolates, a nice dinner," she listed helpfully.

"And don't forget Dorothy Hope's famous mince pies," James added.

Gran took off her apron and hung it on the hook behind the door. "I suppose they're nice enough prizes. But they'd hardly set the world on fire. No, what we need is something really big and tempting."

"But the chocolates *are* tempting," James insisted. "I bet we'll be sold out of tickets in a flash because of them."

Mandy laughed. "That's probably because you plan to buy every ticket yourself to make sure you win them." She pulled on her coat and wrapped her scarf around her neck. "I bet it would be cheaper if you just bought a box," she added mischievously, then darted out the door before James could say anything in reply.

Six

After Mandy and James had pinned up their posters in the supermarket, the post office, and on the bulletin board in the village hall the next morning, they went to Dr. Mason's office to see how Jigsaw and Puzzle were. They were about to go inside when they saw Mrs. Benn crossing the road. To Mandy's surprise, Indy was walking next to her on a leash.

"I knew it," she muttered under her breath.

"Knew what?"

"The novelty's worn off," Mandy said.

James frowned. "What are you talking about?"

"Chloe's lost interest in Indy," Mandy explained, lowering her voice as Mrs. Benn came closer. "Look, her mom's having to look after her now."

"Gee," remarked James. "Do you really think so? I mean, what if Mrs. Benn just felt like taking Indy for a walk?"

"I bet she didn't," Mandy murmured. "Don't you remember her saying the other day that it was Chloe's job?"

"Yes, but —" James began but he had to stop because Mrs. Benn was only yards away from them.

"Hello, you two," she said with a smile. "Coming to visit the rats again, are you?"

"How did you know?" asked Mandy.

"Chloe told me all about them," she said. "She even hinted she'd like one for a pet but since we've gotten Indy, she hasn't even mentioned the word *rat* again." She smiled down at Indy. "I can't say I'm sorry. I'm not sure I'd be too happy about having to take care of a rat as well as this little bundle."

Mandy nudged James but he didn't look at her. Instead he said, "Is Chloe at home?"

Mrs. Benn shook her head. "No. She went to Walton today. One of her school friends called early this morning and invited her to the movies and then to have dinner with her."

"That's nice," Mandy said, meaning it. Chloe deserved

to have some time with her friends. She felt a pang of guilt for having jumped to conclusions, but she couldn't brush away a nagging suspicion that Chloe wasn't exactly over the moon about Indy anymore.

"I thought it would make a nice change for her, too," continued Mrs. Benn. "But I had to practically force her to go. She was worried about leaving Indy all day so I had to promise to puppy-sit as if Indy were a human baby!"

The puppy was sitting quietly at Mrs. Benn's feet, her head drooping so that her long ears brushed against the pavement. This troubled Mandy. *She's looking even less awake than she did yesterday*, she thought uneasily.

As if to answer Mandy's concerns, Mrs. Benn picked up Indy and cuddled her. "You're missing Chloe, aren't you, sweetie?" she said, then to Mandy and James she added, "She's been curled up in her basket ever since Chloe left. I thought some exercise would cheer her up but I don't think it's working. She's more miserable than before we set out so I'm taking her home."

She said good-bye and Mandy and James watched her carry Indy down the street.

"I'm really worried," Mandy said when Mrs. Benn was out of earshot. "There's definitely something odd about Indy."

James shrugged. "She's missing Chloe, like Mrs. Benn said."

"I guess so," Mandy said, "and if that's the problem, then it's not all bad because it shows she and Chloe have bonded well. But I think Indy should have a checkup with Mom and Dad just to make sure she's OK."

"Didn't Sergeant Benn say a vet saw her at the animal shelter in York?" James remembered. He led the way up the steps to Dr. Mason's office.

"Yes, that's right, when he gave the puppies their shots." Mandy pushed down the door handle. "All the same, it won't hurt for Mom and Dad to have a look at her."

In the waiting room, they met Walter Pickard and Ernie Bell, who each lived in one of the small houses behind the Fox and Goose.

"Are you two here for your flu shots, too?" asked Walter. He was sitting on a chair with his flat cloth cap on his lap.

"No. I don't need to have one," said James.

"Me neither," Mandy said. "We've come to see Dr. Mason's rats, Jigsaw and Puzzle. Mom's been treating them for an eye infection."

Ernie Bell frowned, his bushy white eyebrows merging as if they'd been knitted together. "Rats! What's the doctor want to keep a pair of them for? They're nothing but pests."

"Oh, they're not," Mandy insisted. "They're really sweet. And as tame as anything."

"You can train them, you know," put in James.

"What? To keep out of barns?" Ernie said gruffly.

Mandy was used to Ernie's grumpy manner and had learned many years ago to take no notice. Underneath the old man's crusty surface lay a heart of gold.

"Honestly, they're really smart," she persisted. "Jigsaw and Puzzle know their names and they come when Dr. Mason calls them."

"Like pigs can fly," scoffed Ernie. "If you ask me, it's just coincidence. Or they're responding because there's food around. Greedy little creatures. They'll eat anything."

Walter had listened to the exchange with a smile on his face. But now he looked more serious. "Aye, but that's how you can train them. I heard on the radio that scientists have taught rats to sniff out tuberculosis in people even before the doctors can diagnose it. And they do it for the smallest treat, like a raisin. The rats, I mean."

"I didn't think the doctors would do it for a raisin," said Ernie, the corners of his mouth curling up just enough to betray a glimmer of a smile.

Mandy was fascinated. "Did you really hear that?" she asked Walter.

"I did. And it didn't surprise me. I used to have a couple of pet rats, too — Scurry and Scamper." Walter's voice softened. "They were as clever as any creatures I've ever known."

"What happened to them?" asked Ernie, his dark eyes twinkling. "Your cats get them?"

"You old joker, Ernie." Walter laughed. "And for your information, Tom and Scraps came long after the rats passed away."

Mrs. Mason had been busy at her desk but now she looked up and noticed Mandy and James. "I'm sure you're not here to see the doctor." She smiled and, gesturing to the door at the back of the waiting room, said, "Go on up. Jigsaw and Puzzle will be glad to have some company."

"I'd like to see them, too," said Walter. "Do you mind if I go up with Mandy and James?" he asked Mrs. Mason.

"Not at all. But don't be too long. There's only one more patient before you," said the doctor's wife. She looked at Ernie. "Are you going up, too?"

"Why would I want to go and look at some rats?" responded Ernie. "They're just a pair of rodents and the world's overrun with them."

Mandy grimaced. "Don't let Dr. Mason hear you say that. He's crazy about Jigsaw and Puzzle."

"He's crazy to keep 'em." Ernie shrugged and added somberly, "Do you know, you're never more than a few feet away from a rodent?"

"Well, you're certainly not, with Sammy living in your backyard," Walter chuckled. Sammy was Ernie's beloved pet squirrel, who lived in a roomy and impressive run that the former carpenter had made for his unusual animal companion.

Mandy and James burst out laughing.

Ernie looked as if he was about to protest. Then, quite suddenly, he smiled. "In that case, I'd better meet Sammy's distant relatives." He stood up and, ushering Mandy and James ahead of him, said, "Show us the way, you two."

Mandy led everyone upstairs and into the Masons' living room where Jigsaw and Puzzle were peering out inquisitively from their luxury cage. "They must have heard us coming," she said with a chuckle.

She opened the cage so that she and James could reach in. "This one's Puzzle," Mandy said, wrapping her fingers carefully around one sleek-furred tummy and lifting the rat out. She quickly identified the animal by the white splash on her chest.

Puzzle's eyes seemed less watery than before. Mandy tried to look at Jigsaw's but the rat was upside down in one of James's pockets and the only part of her that could be seen was her smooth black tail.

Mandy laughed. "What's she doing in there?"

"Eating dog biscuit crumbs," James said, whose pockets usually held the remains of treats for Blackie.

"As long as she's not eating any raffle tickets," Mandy commented.

"Yikes! There *is* a sheet folded up in there and I've sold about half the tickets," gasped James and he swiftly pulled Jigsaw out.

There was a shred of paper in her mouth.

"Oh, no!" James groaned. He handed Jigsaw to Ernie, then took out the partially nibbled raffle sheet. "That was really stupid of me." He unfolded the paper and Mandy could see that only the edges had been chewed. All the names and telephone numbers were still intact.

"Phew," exclaimed James. "Just in time. I thought we were about to end up with another problem."

"With the raffle, you mean?" asked Walter, looking surprised. He stroked Puzzle, who was sitting quietly in the palm of Mandy's hand, her whiskers and nose twitching.

"Yes. Gran's trying to get decent prizes," Mandy explained. "We've asked lots of people but so far we haven't got anything really exciting."

"Except for the chocolates," added James. He folded up the raffle sheet again and put it back in his pocket.

Walter looked thoughtful. "I wish I had something I could give," he said. He held his hand still and Puzzle slipped onto it from Mandy's palm, then ran up Walter's arm to his shoulder. "If I still had my shop, I could donate a cut of meat or a string of homemade sausages."

Before he retired, Walter had owned the local butcher's shop. "But I can't do that anymore."

Mandy nodded sympathetically, although, as a vegetarian, she was secretly pleased that no meat would find its way onto the list of prizes.

Ernie was stroking Puzzle, who sat quite still in his hand as if she was mesmerized by his stubby fingers. "I wonder what I could give? If Dorothy had asked me some weeks ago, I could have made something." Although he was retired, too, he still did a bit of woodwork from time to time. He looked down fondly at Puzzle and Mandy could tell that the handsome little animal had helped to change Ernie's mind about rats. "So all I can offer really is a lump of wood. But no one's going to want that," he finished.

"Probably not," Mandy agreed.

But James looked as if a thunderbolt had struck him. "Hang on! That's it! You can make something, Mr. Bell. To order. Whoever wins the prize can ask you to make a . . ." He looked around and his eyes fell on the wooden box in Jigsaw and Puzzle's cage. ". . . a box like that one, or . . ." He glanced out of the window. "Or you could offer to mend a fence or a garden shed, or even fix up some furniture."

Ernie's face lit up. "A prize made to order! That's a great idea, James."

"Aye," said Walter and, as if he didn't want to be left out, he added, "I could offer to do something, too. A bit of gardening perhaps, or some decorating."

Mandy thought of what she was best at doing. "I could take people's dogs out for walks, or help to clean out pets' cages during the holidays," she said enthusiastically.

It was the answer to Gran's problem! Instead of giving away objects, people could be asked to give some of their time or skills.

"We'll go home and phone Gran right away. She's going to love the idea," said Mandy.

They returned Jigsaw and Puzzle to their cage and went downstairs where Dr. Mason was looking around for Ernie and Walter.

"Ah, there you are," said the doctor. "I thought you'd run out on us."

"Nope," said Walter. "We were admiring your two lovelies upstairs."

A woman sitting nearby overheard Walter's remark. She looked up from the magazine she was reading and peered disapprovingly at the doctor, Ernie, and Walter.

"He means my pet rats," Dr. Mason quickly explained, and the woman's cold expression changed to one of horror.

"Rats!" She gasped. "In a doctor's office?"

"No. In a cage upstairs in my living room," said the doctor.

But this only made the woman look more shocked. "You have rats in your living room?"

Ernie had started toward the examining room but he stopped in front of the woman and, to Mandy's utter amazement, said, "Yes. And they really are good pets. Clean, loving, and intelligent." He glanced back at the doctor. "Grand companions, too, I should think. A lot like having a squirrel. Only a little easier."

Mandy and James looked at each other and laughed. "That's what happens when you spend some time with an animal and get to know it," Mandy said.

The two friends went to the front door. "Good-bye, Walter, good-bye, Ernie," Mandy said to them over her shoulder. "And thanks for the great idea."

"Go straight home now to tell your gran," Walter replied, looking rather pleased with himself.

"We will," Mandy promised.

Mandy and James left the office and headed back to Animal Ark. On the way, they passed the Benns' house, where they saw a well-muffled figure chasing around in the front yard.

"Hey! There's Chloe," said Mandy, surprised to see

her back so soon. She waved to her as she and James crossed the road. "You're home early, Chloe," she said, stopping at the gate. "We thought you were in Walton."

"I was," said Chloe. "But I decided to come home right after the movie so I could play with Indy." She showed them an old tennis ball. "The trouble is, she doesn't want to do anything." Sure enough, the puppy was lying on the porch with her head between her front paws. "And to think I could have been in the mall shopping with Lucy right now." Chloe sighed and shook her head. "I thought puppies loved to play."

"They do," Mandy said, feeling more puzzled than ever about Indy.

"Maybe she's tired out after her walk with your mom this morning?" James suggested.

Chloe frowned at James. "I don't know how she can be. She's done nothing but sleep since Mom brought her home." She threw the ball onto the porch. It landed with a bounce and rolled toward Indy, who barely noticed it, let alone made any attempt to catch it.

"See what I mean?" said Chloe.

What's even worse than that, Mandy thought, *is that Chloe sounds as if she's losing interest in her.* Just as she had feared on the day that Indy popped out of the apple box, Chloe's excitement at having a puppy was rapidly wearing thin.

"Would you like to bring her to Animal Ark for a checkup?" she suggested, trying to sound tactful.

Chloe shook her head. "Indy's fine. The vet in York saw her before Dad brought her home. And anyway," she continued, "Mom's so busy trying to cope with Harvey in the hospital, she'd probably flip her lid if I started making a fuss about Indy."

Mandy couldn't argue with that. But when she looked at Indy again and saw the forlorn expression on the puppy's gentle golden face, she felt a lump form in her throat. It wasn't even Christmas yet, but already Indy had the look of an unloved, unwanted, and completely unsuitable Christmas gift.

Seven

"It'll be the most unique raffle yet." Gran chuckled when she heard James's idea for the prizes. She'd arrived at Animal Ark with yet another batch of mince pies at the same time as Mandy and James.

"Yes, you've certainly come up with a winner," said Dr. Emily, filling the kettle and switching it on. Both she and Dr. Adam had a gap between appointments so they had come into the kitchen for a cup of tea and a piece of mince pie.

James looked pleased. "We should end up with some really cool prizes."

"Unless, of course, people offer some very weird

skills," Dr. Adam grinned. "I mean, it's all right if you win Gran to bake for you every day," he teased, "but imagine winning Mrs. Ponsonby for an afternoon of singing?"

Mrs. Ponsonby was a large, bossy woman with a voice like a foghorn. She was in the church choir and her voice always boomed out loudly above all the others.

"That would be painful," Mandy agreed. "We'll just have to be careful who we ask."

"Let's think about who we *should* approach," said James. He took a pencil out of a jar on the table and a used envelope from the recycling bin. He wrote down Ernie's and Walter's names and their offers, then, biting the top of the pencil, looked at the others. "Any ideas?"

"We could ask Mrs. Ponsonby to act as a foghorn for the person who wins the rowing boat ride." Dr. Adam laughed, pouring the boiling water into the teapot.

"Really, Adam!" tutted Gran, who was arranging some of the mince pies on a plate. "Be serious."

"I am," he said and straightened his face with an effort. "OK, then. I'll start the ball rolling and offer . . ." He paused and Mandy assumed he'd come up with his usual offer of a vet check. ". . . to clean out someone's garage."

Mandy looked at her father in astonishment. "You *hate* cleaning out the garage!"

"That's why it's such a generous offer," her dad responded.

"How on earth do I compete with that?" Dr. Emily smiled. She rested her chin in her hand and gazed out the window. "I know," she said after a while. "I could offer to wash and polish someone's car."

Dr. Adam looked as if he'd been struck dumb. "*You* wash a car?" he exclaimed, raising his eyebrows. "This I have to see."

"You will." Dr. Emily grinned. "And you'll be surprised how good I am at it."

Gran and James came up with a few suggestions, too.

"What about Bill Ward?" said James. Bill was the local mailman. "I bet there's all kind of things he could do." He made a note of his name while Gran came up with another possibility.

"I'll ask my friend Marion Timpson," she said. "Seeing as she works at the hospital she'll want to support the raffle, I'm sure. She might offer to sit with someone when they're ill."

"Or babysit for a couple so they can go out," said Dr. Emily, pouring out three cups of tea.

"That'll be a popular prize." Dr. Adam grinned, helping himself to two pieces of mince pie which made Gran look sternly at him. "A bossy matron would be an ideal babysitter. The kids wouldn't dare step out of line."

"Marion's a very nice person," said Grandma Hope. "You're full of banter today, aren't you?"

"It must be something you've put in the mince pies!" Dr. Adam joked.

Throughout the good-natured teasing, Mandy said nothing. She sat with her elbows on the table and her head in her hands, thinking only of Indy. The image of the little puppy looking lost and unloved kept swimming back into her mind.

"I know someone else who could do with a dose of whatever's in those mince pies," remarked Dr. Emily. "She's looking rather down in the mouth today."

Mandy realized her mom meant her. "I'm OK," she said, sitting up straighter. "I'm just a little worried about Indy."

"Chloe's new pup?" asked Dr. Emily. "Why?"

"It sounds strange, but she's not full of beans like a puppy should be. And I think Chloe's getting tired of her," Mandy explained.

"Surely not?" said Gran. "Those two are the best of friends."

James had been studying the list of names on the envelope but now he looked up and said, "You wouldn't have thought so about half an hour ago." He described the failed playing session that he and Mandy had seen in the Benns' front yard. "Like Mandy said, Chloe was really fed up," he finished.

"I wouldn't read too much into that," said Dr. Emily, standing up and taking her white coat off the back of her chair.

But Mandy couldn't ignore the wave of anxiety building up in her. "Honestly, Mom," she persisted, "something's wrong! I just can't put my finger on it. Couldn't you and Dad visit the Benns and take a look at Indy? Please?"

Dr. Emily slipped on the vet's coat. "We can't show up at someone's home and insist on examining their dog." She pulled her long red hair out from beneath her collar. "I'm sure if the Benns are worried about Indy they'll bring her to Animal Ark."

"That's just it," Mandy said, following her mom to the door. "Chloe won't ask her mom to bring her because she says she's got too much to worry about with Harvey being ill."

"She's got a point," said Dr. Adam, gulping down the last mouthful of tea before following Dr. Emily out to the clinic. "Mrs. Benn has to cope with a lot right now." He stopped to put an arm around Mandy. "Relax, love. Indy will be fine. If the vet who saw her in York was happy with her, I don't think we can interfere." He turned Mandy to face him and, with his hands on her shoulders, he said solemnly, "You're looking for problems that aren't there. Just because Indy's a Christmas present, it doesn't mean she's going to end up being neglected."

Mandy sighed. Her dad knew her only too well. "I suppose so," she said. "But I still wish you'd have a look at her."

Dr. Adam smiled. "You don't give up, do you?" He pushed an arm through one of the sleeves of his white coat and, fumbling for the other so that Mandy had to help him, he added, "All right then. If the opportunity comes up, we'll check that little pup."

"Thanks, Dad," said Mandy. She looked at James and gave him a tiny nod. Her mind was already working out how to make sure this opportunity came up.

Later that day, Mandy and James were sweeping out the residential unit when Chloe called. When Mandy heard who it was on the phone, she was immediately filled with a burst of hope. *I bet she's decided to bring Indy in after all*, she thought.

But Mandy's imagination was working overtime. Chloe didn't even mention Indy. Instead, she had phoned to say that Harvey was coming home from the hospital the next morning. "He's much better," she said, relief in her voice.

Mandy was pleased for her. "So you'll be having Christmas after all?"

"I hope so. But Harvey has to be kept quiet so I'm going to have to think of ways to entertain him," said Chloe.

Mandy's immediate thought was that Indy would have been perfect at keeping Harvey amused, if only she'd been a perky, playful puppy. But then she remembered the little boy's reaction when Indy knocked over his toy garage. He obviously didn't like dogs all that much. *It's probably just as well Indy's quietened down,* Mandy told herself. Another scene like that would defi-

nitely put the little spaniel on Mrs. Benn's bad side and wouldn't help Harvey one bit.

Chloe was still talking about her brother. "He's really skinny because he isn't eating very well, and he has to have some icky yellow medicine every day. He hates it and kicks up a huge fuss when the nurses appear with the drug cart."

"Poor Harvey," Mandy sympathized. "It's horrible having to swallow something that tastes awful."

"Well, that's just too bad," responded Chloe, sounding unusually hard-hearted. "The medicine's helping him to get better so he'll have to put up with it."

"I suppose so," Mandy said, thinking of the times she'd helped her mom and dad to give reluctant animals their medicine. She was tempted to ask how Indy was but thought better of it and asked instead if she and James could visit Harvey when he came home.

"Yes, please," Chloe said at once. "I'm sure he'd love to see you."

After Mandy hung up, she went back to the residential unit where James was sitting on the floor playing with a small black mutt who'd been brought in as a stray a few hours before. Luckily, the dog's owners had been traced from the microchip implanted under the dog's skin, and they were coming to get him after work.

Mandy sat down next to James. "Harvey's coming

home from the hospital tomorrow morning," she told him. "I thought we could go by and see him in the afternoon."

"OK," said James. He'd rolled his hand into a tight fist with a dog treat inside and was holding it on the ground in front of the little mutt, who pawed at it, trying to make him open it. "You'll have to do better than that if you want the treat." James chuckled.

The dog, whose name was Ebony, sat up straight and barked.

"OK, OK." James laughed. "You said please, so you can have it." He opened his hand.

Ebony pounced upon the bone-shaped biscuit, crunched it up in a flash, then sat up again, gazing expectantly at James.

"Who's a lucky pup?" said Mandy fondly. She patted Ebony as James fished another biscuit out of his pocket.

"Yeah. He'll do practically anything to get a treat," said James. He covered his pocket with his hand because Ebony had realized where the source of the treats was and had begun to nose them out for himself, his ears pricked and his tail wagging at top speed.

"I wish that would work for Indy," Mandy said wistfully.

James took off his glasses to wipe them on his shirt. "Are you still worried about her?" he asked, quickly putting his hand back over his pocket as Ebony pushed his small black nose in to help himself to more biscuits.

Mandy scratched Ebony behind his ears. "Yes. You've seen her. She doesn't look right. And I don't know if that's because she's feeling neglected or bored, or if she's unsettled because of all the coming and going in the Benns' house."

"Don't you think you're looking for things that aren't there, like your dad said?" James warned, putting his glasses back on.

"No, I don't," Mandy said firmly. "But at least we'll be able to see her again when we visit Harvey tomorrow." She set her mouth in a tight line and James shook his head resignedly, as if he knew better than to argue with her when she was being this determined.

They arrived at the Benns' house the next afternoon armed with puzzles and coloring books. It was a bright, cold day and Blackie had come with them so James tied him to a railing on the porch.

"We won't be long," he promised.

Blackie wagged his tail as if he understood, then sat down with a patient expression on his face.

Mandy reached up to ring the bell but at that same moment, a loud wailing came from inside. She hesitated and glanced back at James. "I wonder what's going on?" she said. Then she heard Harvey yelling, "I don't want it. It's horrible!"

"Must be time for his medicine," she guessed, deciding not to ring the bell until the screaming was over.

"Take it away," Harvey shouted.

Just then, the front door opened and Chloe appeared with Indy in her arms. "I was looking out the window and saw you coming," she explained above the ear-piercing yells. She stepped onto the porch and closed the door behind her. "We always have a screaming match when Harvey has to take his medicine. It's really awful so I thought we'd take Indy out for a walk and come back when Harvey's calmed down."

"Good idea," said James. "Blackie would love to show Indy all his favorite sniffing places."

Mandy and James put the books and puzzles they'd brought for Harvey on a chair just inside the hall and then, with Chloe still carrying Indy, they set off down the road and turned into a quiet street that led away from the village.

"Why don't you put Indy down now?" Mandy suggested to Chloe. There wasn't much point in taking a dog for a walk if it was carried all the way. "There's no traffic here so it's quite safe for her."

"Sure," said Chloe, lowering the puppy to the ground. "But she probably won't walk very far. She doesn't like going out."

"Don't worry, Blackie will get her going," said James, watching his dog romp along ahead of them, stopping every so often to sniff at a hedge or tree trunk.

Apparently surprised to find herself on the ground, Indy looked up at Chloe, then started padding slowly behind her. Not for the first time, Mandy was struck by how skinny the puppy was, even though her tummy was really bloated. *Maybe she's not getting the right food*, she wondered, and made a mental note to find out what Chloe was feeding her.

A sudden commotion at the end of the street made Mandy forget about Indy for a moment. Blackie had spotted a duck and chased it into the hedge. The distressed duck was quacking loudly from somewhere among the branches while Blackie, who must have thought this was the best game in the world, barked and bounced around in a frenzy of excitement.

"He's cornered the poor thing," James gasped, setting off at a run to rescue the duck. "Blackie, heel!" he ordered, his words wasted as Blackie ignored him and continued trying to flush the unfortunate duck out from the hedge.

"He's quite a handful," remarked Chloe, and she looked back at Indy as if to point out the contrast between the two dogs.

Mandy glanced back, too. To her dismay, Indy had stopped in a puddle in the middle of the road and was being sick.

"Oh, no! Not again," muttered Chloe and the impatient note in her voice revived all of Mandy's concerns about whether the puppy was really wanted at all.

"It's OK," Mandy said quickly and hurried back to Indy. "Puppies do get sick." And although she was telling the truth because she often saw dogs eating grass to administer their own medicine for a sore tummy, her words sounded hollow. *It's* not *OK*, she told herself. She was sure that all the signs pointed to something a lot more serious than just a sore tummy. But she had no idea what that could be.

By the time Mandy reached Indy, the puppy had stopped being sick and was sitting helplessly in the puddle, her golden coat damp and muddy.

"You poor baby," Mandy whispered and bent to pick her up.

But Chloe ran up behind her and put her hands around the little spaniel's middle first. "Look at the mess you've made of yourself," she said, sounding annoyed as she picked up Indy. "Mom's going to hit the roof when she sees you."

Indy gazed at Chloe with huge mournful eyes and licked her hand.

"It's like she's saying she's sorry," Mandy murmured, feeling her throat tighten. The puppy adored her owner no matter what.

Chloe said nothing. She tucked Indy under one arm and turned away, but not before Mandy saw a tear rolling down her cheek.

Eight

"It's not the end of the world," Mandy said, trying to comfort Chloe. "We can easily wash Indy off."

"I know," Chloe said. "But Mom will be upset all the same, especially if Indy brings mud indoors."

James had managed to clip the leash onto Blackie's collar and pull him away from the duck. "She doesn't have to know," he said. "We can bathe Indy at my house. It's not far from here, and my mom's so used to Blackie coming home covered in mud, she won't notice another dirty dog. Especially such a tiny one." He patted Indy's head. "We'll have you cleaned up in a flash."

Behind them, Mandy saw the duck waddle cautiously

94

out from the hedge. It paused and looked around, then suddenly ran forward, its wings beating fast. Blackie had seen it, too. He strained at the leash, barking frantically.

Taken by surprise, James found the leash jerked out of his hand. "Hey! Come back here, Blackie!" he yelled.

But Blackie was deaf to James's command and hurtled toward the duck. This time, though, the bird had the advantage. Before Blackie could reach it, it took off and flew directly over the Labrador, its wings working hard to keep its heavy body airborne.

As if he was catching a Frisbee, Blackie leaped vertically into the air, swiveling around as the duck flew over him. But he missed it by a long way and hit the ground hard, landing in a muddy ditch next to the road. When he emerged a second later, he was no longer black, but dirty brown and very wet.

"See what I mean?" James said to Chloe. "That makes two of them that need a bath." He strode across to Blackie, who looked rather embarrassed. His tail hung limply and he held his head low as he blinked guiltily up at his owner.

"You silly dog!" James scolded, picking up the mud-coated leash. But there was resignation and wry amusement in his voice.

That was all the encouragement Blackie needed. He jumped up on James and gleefully licked his face.

"You're impossible." James laughed, pushing the dog down and looking through his mud-splattered glasses at his equally muddy clothes. "Thanks very much," he said, trying to sound stern.

"That makes *three* of you who need a bath." Mandy chuckled.

Chloe had begun to look more cheerful. "Well, Indy, you're about to have your first bath and it looks like it's going to be in a pretty crowded tub!" She grinned.

At James's house, they went straight to the laundry room where there was a big double sink. When Mrs. Hunter saw the two muddy dogs and her disheveled son, she merely raised her eyebrows and said, "Boys and dogs," then took out a couple of old towels and put them on the radiator. "Make sure you dry that little pup properly after her bath," she said. On her way out, she glanced at Blackie and added, "And keep that fellow in here until he's completely clean!"

James ordered Blackie to sit by the door while he half filled the sink with warm water. "Indy first," he said, and Chloe lowered the puppy into the water while Mandy stood by with one of the towels.

Indy was as good as gold and sat absolutely still while Chloe rinsed the mud off her. When the puppy was clean, Chloe lifted her out of the sink. Dripping wet and with her coat clinging to her, Indy looked even thinner than Mandy had first thought. She almost said something, but bit her lip. Chloe had been upset enough earlier so it probably wasn't the right time to raise the subject of the puppy's diet.

Chloe handed the pup to Mandy, who wrapped her in the towel. "There. You're as good as new," she said, gently rubbing her dry and wincing as she felt Indy's ribs sticking out. She peeled off the towel and tossed it into the laundry basket while cuddling the puppy close to keep her warm.

Indy looked up at her with soft brown eyes. Mandy expected her to wriggle, wanting to get down, but Indy seemed quite content to stay where she was.

Meanwhile, James was preparing to wash the mud off Blackie. "He'll have to stand on one of the towels and I'll sponge him off," he said. "He's far too big to fit in the sink." He filled a bucket with warm water, then looked around for his dog.

But Blackie had vanished.

"Now where's he gone to?" said James. He went into the kitchen and Mandy heard him exclaim, "You bad boy!"

Mandy and Chloe looked through the door to see what was going on. Blackie was lying under the kitchen table with his ears flat against his head as if he was trying to be invisible. Clearly, he'd seen what had hap-

pened to Indy and had decided he wasn't going to have
a bath as well.

"You can't escape." James chuckled. He crawled under the table, grabbed Blackie by the collar, and
dragged him out, leaving a muddy smear behind them.
"Just as well Mom's not in here to see this," he said.

"You'd better clean it up before she does come in,"
said Mandy. She passed Indy back to Chloe and took
the Labrador from James to steer him back into the
laundry room.

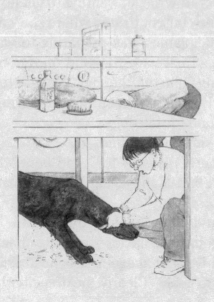

By the time both dogs were clean and dry, it was almost dinnertime. Mandy didn't think it would be a good idea for them all to turn up at Chloe's house, as Harvey could be in bed by now, so they postponed their visit till the morning. "But give him the coloring books and puzzles from us," she said to Chloe as she was leaving.

After Chloe and her newly washed pup had gone, Mandy suggested to James that they visit Gran to see if she'd had any luck with more donations for the raffle. "She won't mind unexpected visitors at dinnertime," she said, knowing how delighted Gran always was to see her and James.

Mandy had left her bicycle at James's house earlier and the two of them wheeled their bikes down the path to the front gate. Mr. Hunter arrived home just as they were leaving. He parked his car in the driveway and waved to them before taking a few packages out of the trunk. One of them was a plastic envelope marked PC CONNECTION.

James nudged Mandy. "Looks promising," he said.

"Do you think that software you want for Christmas is in there?" Mandy asked.

"What else could it be?" he replied confidently. "Looks like I'll getting my holiday wish this year!"

They went through the gate, then biked the short distance to Lilac Cottage.

As Mandy had predicted, Gran was only too happy to rustle up some food for them, especially as she was on her own. Grandpa had gone fishing with a friend.

"I'll have something ready in a jiff," Dorothy Hope promised, and before long they were sitting at the kitchen table eating grilled cheese and tomato sandwiches while going through the list of prizes.

"Bill Ward said he'd repair broken bicycles," said Gran, pointing to the mailman's name on the list. "And Marion Timpson's going to give first-aid lessons. I also spoke to Myra Hugill, the fair Chairman, and she's offered to teach cross-stitch."

James made a face. "Gee, I hope I don't win that prize. What is cross-stitch, anyway?"

"It's a type of embroidery," Gran told him, and James looked even more horrified.

Mandy had to admit that it wasn't exactly the sort of prize she'd like to win, either. "But some people love sewing and at least it's a prize," she pointed out.

"Well, if I win it, I'll donate it right back," said James.

"Big talk from someone who hasn't come up with an offer himself," said Gran pointedly.

"Oops!" James gulped. "I was too busy thinking of what other people could give." He narrowed his eyes. "Let's see," he murmured thoughtfully. "What can I . . ."

Suddenly, he snapped his fingers. "Got it! I can offer computer lessons."

"An excellent idea." Gran beamed, writing down James's name and his offer on the list.

"Well, that's another prize I definitely don't want to win," Mandy teased.

James pretended to be hurt. "It's just as good a prize as the one you're offering," he said and helped himself to another grilled sandwich. "If I don't win the chocolates, I wouldn't mind winning your dog-walking services. After Blackie's behavior this afternoon, I don't feel like ever taking him out again."

"What did he do?" asked Gran, looking intrigued.

James recounted the incident with the duck, which made Gran laugh heartily. "What did little Indy think of it all?" she asked.

"Not much," Mandy said glumly. "I don't think she even saw the duck."

Gran looked surprised. "A spaniel not see a duck! That's odd. Breeds like that should see a bird from miles away."

"Indy's still very young," James reminded her.

"Maybe so," said Gran. "But I still think she should have reacted in some way."

"So do I," Mandy agreed.

Gran frowned at her and said, "You're convinced there's a problem with that puppy, aren't you?"

Mandy nodded. "And I'm worried that because Indy's not exactly a bundle of fun, Chloe's on the verge of giving up on her."

"That's the problem with pets as Christmas presents," said Gran, echoing Mandy's secret fear. "Once the novelty has worn off, they're often left on the sidelines."

"That's not going to happen to Indy, if there's anything I can do about it," Mandy said with determination.

There was the sound of an engine outside, and Mandy glanced out the window to see Grandpa coming up the driveway in his camper van.

"About time, too," said Gran, switching on the toaster oven. "I'll have to start making grilled sandwiches all over again."

"I'll do them," Mandy offered.

"That's all right, dear." Gran smiled, picking up the bread knife and slicing into a fresh loaf. "I'd probably have had to make some more anyway." She looked at James. "Wouldn't I?"

James shrugged guiltily. "Well, they were delicious," he said, as a roundabout way of saying he would like more.

A few minutes later, Grandpa came in through the kitchen door. "Here you are, love," he said, putting two fish-shaped parcels wrapped in newspaper on the counter. "Tomorrow's lunch."

Mandy wasn't too keen on the idea of fishing. Fish were animals, too, and she couldn't bear anything to be killed or hurt. "It's mean to go hunting for other creatures and eat them," she scolded her grandfather.

"Does the same thing apply when the fish eat these?" he said and, with a mischievous glint in his eyes, he put a plastic container on the table in front of Mandy. It was full of squirming pink worms.

But instead of recoiling in disgust as Grandpa obviously expected her to, Mandy stared at the slimy worms for a moment before leaping to her feet. "Worms! That's it," she cried, as James looked at her in astonishment. "That's what's wrong with Indy!"

Nine

Even though it was nearly dark, Mandy pedaled back to Animal Ark like someone trying to win the Tour de France.

Riding a few paces behind her, James called out, "Hang on, Mandy. Worms can't be all that serious."

"Yes, they can," Mandy shouted back over her shoulder. "Indy could die."

"No way!"

"Yes way!" Mandy yelled as she whizzed under the wooden Animal Ark sign and raced to the clinic at the back. She slammed on her brakes so that the bike skidded sideways and leaped off, letting the bike drop to the ground. Gasping for breath, she ran up the stairs and pushed open the door that led into the reception area.

"Where are Mom and Dad?" she blurted out to Jean Knox, who was getting ready to go home.

"And hello to you, too, Mandy," said Jean, taking her car keys out of her handbag and snapping it shut.

"Sorry. But it's an emergency." Mandy puffed, heading toward her mom's examining room.

"It always is with you." Jean smiled, sliding the bag over her forearm before switching off the lamp on her desk. "Oh, and if you're looking for your mom," she added as Mandy pushed down the door handle, "she's . . ."

"Not there," Mandy said, looking into the empty room.

"As I was saying, your mom and dad have finished for the day. They're in the cottage," Jean continued.

"Oh, right," Mandy said. She was about to go through the door that connected the clinic with the old stone cottage where the Hopes lived when James came in, looking very disheveled. There was a rip in his jeans just above one knee, his coat was smeared with dirt and he had a small gash on one cheek.

"What happened to you?" Mandy asked in amazement. In her haste, she hadn't noticed that he wasn't right behind her when she came into the clinic.

"I fell off at the end of the driveway," he admitted sheepishly. He picked a twig out of his hair. "Now my front wheel's a little buckled."

"Oh, well, as long as you're OK," was Mandy's only reaction. Her mind was still fixed on Indy and the chance that the puppy was chronically ill from worms.

"Thanks for the sympathy," muttered James, following her through the door.

They found Mandy's parents in front of the fire in the living room. Dr. Emily had been wrapping Christmas presents. As soon as she saw them, she quickly pushed a squashy-looking package behind one of the cushions on the sofa.

"What's up?" asked Dr. Adam. His eyes grew wide when he saw James. "Have you been in a fight?"

"No. I —"

"Indy's seriously ill," Mandy burst out, interrupting James.

"Hold on, hold on," said Dr. Adam. "One at a time."

"It's nothing. I just fell off my bike."

"I think Indy's full of worms."

The explanations came one on top of the other.

Mandy's parents exchanged looks. "Did you get that, Emily?" asked Dr. Adam.

"I think so." She nodded. "James took a fall and

Mandy's diagnosed Indy with worms." She stood up and went to James. "Let me have a look at this cut on your cheek. And, Mandy, tell us more about your diagnosis."

"Well, you know how Indy's been so tired and doesn't want to play?" Mandy began. "And she's also quite thin with a potbelly?"

"That doesn't automatically mean worms," warned her dad. He folded up the newspaper he'd been reading and tossed it onto the coffee table.

"No, but she's also had an upset tummy and we saw her being sick this afternoon," Mandy continued. Dr. Adam frowned as if he found these symptoms more convincing.

"Hold that thought for a minute," said Dr. Emily. "I'm going to get some ointment for this cut." She went into the kitchen and came back a few moments later with a first-aid kit. "You were saying, Mandy?"

"Well, Chloe mentioned that Indy had been sick before and she also said that she isn't eating much. So when I saw Grandpa's can of worms —"

"You put two and two together . . ." began Dr. Adam.

"And made four," finished his wife. She unscrewed the lid from a tube of antibiotic cream and, with James looking a bit embarrassed, dabbed it on his cheek. "There. You shouldn't have any trouble with that," she told him, then looked at Mandy. "You know, love, I think you might be on the right track. Diarrhea, vomiting, list-lessness, poor appetite — that all points to worms."

Adam Hope was leaning forward in his chair. "And when you take the puppy's history into account, it makes further sense. If her mother was a stray, she was probably malnourished and Indy could have contracted worms from her even before she was born."

James had been listening with a puzzled frown on his face. "But I thought Chloe's dad said a vet in York had checked Indy. Wouldn't he have wormed her at the same time?"

"I expect he did," said Dr. Emily, returning the oint-ment to the first-aid box. "But if Indy was already rid-dled with worms, one dose of medicine wouldn't have done the trick."

"But how bad can worms be?" asked James. "I mean, can they really kill a puppy?" He touched the cut on his cheek with his fingertips, then stopped and lowered his hand when Dr. Emily shook her head at him and mouthed, "Leave it alone."

"Absolutely," said Mandy's dad grimly. "In young pup-pies, worms can cause an obstruction in the bowel as well as serious anemia."

James frowned. "That's something to do with the blood, isn't it?"

"That's right," said Dr. Emily. "It means the red blood

cells aren't working properly." She closed the first-aid box and put it on the coffee table, pushing aside some rolls of wrapping paper to make room for it. "Worms also absorb a lot of the goodness from the food a puppy eats, which means that the pup doesn't get all the nourishment it needs."

"Which explains why Indy's so thin and has no energy," Mandy put in. With her mom and dad agreeing that Indy was probably in big trouble, her anxiety grew even more urgent. "We've got to treat her fast. She's weak enough already."

Dr. Emily was on her way to the hall even before Mandy had finished speaking. "You're right, Mandy. But first we'll need to run some tests to see exactly what we're dealing with. I'll phone Shula Benn and arrange to see Indy as soon as possible."

Everyone clustered around Dr. Emily while she made the call. Mandy could tell that her mom didn't want to alarm the family too much because she didn't go into any detail.

"Shula, I know you're pressed for time right now and it's difficult for you to bring Indy in for a routine checkup," said Dr. Emily in a calm, friendly voice. "So I wondered if you'd like me to come by and take a look at her? We've been trying to think of something we could do to help you and came up with this idea."

Mandy held her breath as she waited for the answer.

"Good, then we'll see you after breakfast tomorrow," Dr. Emily said at last, with a thumbs-up at Mandy and James.

Mandy leaned against the wall and breathed out with relief, even though she wished they could go examine Indy right away. The longer it was before the pup was seen, the more chance there would be of serious complications developing. And Mandy couldn't bear it if Chloe lost her adorable Christmas present.

"Don't mention that we suspect Indy is in a bad way. We don't want to upset Chloe," Dr. Emily warned Mandy when she parked the Animal Ark Land Rover outside the Benns' house the next morning. James wasn't with them as he was preparing his computer course for the raffle. But he'd made Mandy promise to call him the moment she got back from seeing Indy.

"OK. But what if she wants to know why we're taking tests, or if Indy's so bad she has to come to the residential unit for a while?" Mandy asked.

"We'll just have to play the whole thing by ear," said Dr. Emily, ringing the doorbell.

Chloe answered it a moment later. "It's nice of you to come and see my puppy," she said when she opened the door.

"Is she OK?" Mandy couldn't help asking as Chloe led the way into the living room.

"Same as ever. Sleeping most of the time," Chloe replied.

Harvey was propped up on the sofa with a tray on his lap. On it was one of the jigsaw puzzles that Mandy and James had brought for him the day before — a colorful picture of tractors and farmyard animals. The little boy was still pale and thin, but he looked a lot more cheerful than the last time Mandy had seen him.

"Hi, Harvey. Feeling better?" Mandy asked, glancing around to see if Indy was there, too.

"A little," said Harvey, slotting in a puzzle piece. "Where's James?"

"He had to stay behind to do some work on his computer. I'm sure he'd have much rather come here," Mandy told Harvey. But what she didn't say was that James's real reason for wanting to be there would have been the same as hers, to see how Indy was.

Mrs. Benn came in carrying a large brown bottle of medicine. As soon as Harvey saw it, he covered his face with his hands. "No, Mommy! Take it away!" he cried.

Shula Benn sighed and shook her head. "We have the same performance every time," she told Dr. Emily. "You'd think I was poisoning him. Excuse me a moment." She sat down on the sofa next to Harvey and

poured out a spoonful of the thick yellow medicine. "Come on now, Harvey. Show everyone how brave you are."

Harvey kept his hands firmly over his mouth and shook his head. "Don't want it," he mumbled.

"That's too bad," said his mom with a trace of impatience. "You *have* to have it."

Chloe bent over the back of the sofa and said cheerfully, "You want to be better for Christmas, don't you?"

Harvey nodded but kept his mouth well-covered.

"If you don't take your medicine, you won't be well. You could even end up in the hospital again," Chloe went on.

"Don't want it," Harvey whined and coughed chestily.

While this was going on, Mandy was looking around for Indy. When she couldn't see the pup, her anxiety got the better of her. "Where's Indy?" she found herself blurting out.

"In her bed, I think," said Chloe, then went back to encouraging her brother to open his mouth.

In her bed, you think! Mandy couldn't believe how casual Chloe was about the little dog. She shot her mom a worried look but Dr. Emily just made a tiny movement of her head. *Hold fire,* she seemed to be saying, and Mandy reminded herself that Chloe didn't know just how sick Indy might be.

Dr. Emily put her vet's bag on a side table, then sat down in an armchair and indicated with a nod that Mandy should do the same.

But Mandy couldn't have sat still for all the dog sweaters in the world. She was too on edge about Indy to be able to relax.

Meanwhile, Chloe and her mom were having no success with Harvey.

"Now stop this, Harvey," said his mother angrily. She tried to pull his hands away from his mouth but he turned his head away from Mrs. Benn.

"Here, let me try," volunteered Chloe, and she took the spoon from her mother and said to Harvey, "If you swallow it, I'll spend the whole afternoon playing Chutes and Ladders with you."

"That'll be fun," remarked Mandy, trying to sound encouraging.

"Don't want to play Chutes and Ladders," Harvey said through clenched teeth.

"All right, then, we'll play cars," Chloe tried again, irritation creeping into her voice. "Come on, Harv. Just open your mouth and swallow fast. You'll hardly taste the stuff."

Harvey turned his face away again. "Take it away," he moaned. "It's horrible."

Jeepers! This could go on for hours, Mandy thought, giving her mom another frustrated look. And all the while, Indy, wherever she was, needed just as much attention as Harvey was getting. Mandy was about to ask if she could go find the pup when her eyes fell on the toy garage on the floor. That gave her an idea. "You know what, Harvey?" she said, crouching down next to the sofa. "I think the doctors have got it all wrong."

Harvey looked at Mandy with his eyes wide.

Mandy went on, "You see, I think that what's really the matter with you is that you've run out of gas."

Harvey bit his bottom lip but he couldn't stop the corners of his mouth from curling into a smile.

"So we need to fill up your tank," Mandy said. She reached for one of the toy gas pumps and held the tiny hose in front of Harvey's face. "I'm sure cars think that gas tastes horrible," she said. "But it makes them go. And at this garage, you get a special-tasting gas so it's not nearly as bad as the other kind." She looked at Chloe. "Fill him up," she said.

For a second, Mandy thought Harvey wasn't going to cooperate, but when Chloe brought the spoon up to him again, he opened his mouth and, without even making a face, swallowed the yellow syrup.

Chloe and her mom gave Mandy a grateful look. "You've just become Harvey's unofficial nurse." Chloe grinned.

"Actually, I'm supposed to be Indy's unofficial nurse," Mandy said, nearly bursting with impatience. There was still no sign of the puppy and Mandy pictured her lying limply somewhere in the house, ignored and perhaps even forgotten. "You know, for the checkup that mom's going to give her?"

"Oh, right," said Chloe, as if the puppy was the last thing on her mind. "I'll go and find her."

While Chloe was out of the room, Dr. Emily asked Mrs. Benn how the puppy's appetite was.

"She's a picky eater, that's for sure," answered Mrs. Benn. "A lot like Harvey, really."

Without thinking, Mandy blurted out, "That's probably because Indy's sick, too."

Her outburst coincided with Chloe coming back into the living room carrying Indy. "What did you say?" Chloe asked at the same time that Harvey said, "Indy's run out of gas."

Chloe looked completely shocked. She stared at Mandy, then down at the puppy in her arms. "What did you say?" she repeated hoarsely.

Rats! Mandy thought, wishing she'd kept quiet as her mom had suggested. But there was no way out of it now. She'd have to explain everything. "Look, Chloe," she began, leaning forward to pat the little dog. "Indy's not well. And I'm sure you know it."

Chloe's reaction took her completely by surprise. "You've got real nerve, Mandy Hope," she said angrily. "Just because your mom and dad are vets, it doesn't mean you know everything about animals."

Mandy opened her mouth to speak but Chloe didn't

give her the chance. "Like I told you, Indy's fine. And you should mind your own business."

"But . . ." Mandy tried again.

Chloe wasn't listening. She dumped Indy in her mom's lap, then spun around and rushed out of the room, slamming the door behind her.

Mandy felt stunned. Chloe had been so patient and caring with Harvey, but she was completely the opposite when it came to Indy. She looked helplessly at her mom and said, "I didn't mean to upset Chloe. I'll go and tell her I'm sorry." She went toward the door but Mrs. Benn stopped her.

"Leave her. She'll be all right once she's calmed down." Handing Indy to Mandy's mom, she added, "But I hope you're wrong about Indy not being well. That's the last thing we need."

Mandy could only agree with her. Seeing the skinny little puppy sitting forlornly on her mom's lap, she felt all her misgivings about Christmas pets come flooding back. And on top of that, Indy had been brought into a home that simply didn't have time for her right now.

Ten

Back at Animal Ark an hour later, Mandy sat on a tall stool at her mom's lab table, watching Dr. Emily peer through her microscope at the samples she'd taken from Indy. Dr. Emily had explained to Mrs. Benn that Indy might have worms but that she'd need to take tests before she knew for sure.

The news had come as a shock to Mrs. Benn but she was grateful that Mandy had been persistent in trying to figure out why Indy was so lethargic.

"See anything?" Mandy asked her mom. She leaned forward with her elbows on the table and her chin in her hands.

"Oh, yes indeed," said Dr. Emily. She adjusted the lens and studied the sample on the slide for a few more seconds before looking up at Mandy. "You were right to trust your intuition, honey. Indy's riddled with roundworm. Take a look." She moved aside so that Mandy could get to the microscope.

Mandy bent over the eyepiece and peered at the squiggly shapes on the slide. They looked a lot like miniature earthworms. "Horrible things," she said, her love for animals not extending to the parasitic creatures in front of her.

Dr. Emily took the slide out from under the microscope and rinsed it under the faucet, then put it into the autoclave to be sterilized along with other instruments. "At least we know what we're dealing with now. We'll give her some deworming tablets right away. She can have a dose today, then another in about seven days. And, of course, Chloe will have to keep an eye on her in case the worms come back."

Sounds easy enough, thought Mandy, although she wasn't too sure about the last piece of her mom's instructions. Chloe had ignored all the symptoms before, and she'd acted really strangely when she'd heard that Indy was sick. What chance was there that she'd take her blinders off and notice if the puppy got sick again?

The door opened and Dr. Adam popped his head in. "Everything all right?"

"Indy's got roundworm," Mandy announced.

"Poor little puppy," said Dr. Adam. "No wonder she's so miserable. But at least we know for sure what's up with her. All that's thanks to you, Mandy."

"It wasn't hard to see that she was off color," Mandy said modestly.

"I don't know about that," said her dad. "I mean, you were the only one who noticed, like the best sort of vet would."

Mandy felt pleased. The best compliment anyone could pay her was to say she had the makings of a good vet.

"Are the Benns coming by for the medicine?" Dr. Adam continued. He looked over his shoulder at the crowded waiting room.

"I'll take it to them," Mandy offered, realizing it would be hard for both her mom and Mrs. Benn to get away right then. They both had patients depending on them, animals in Dr. Emily's case, and Harvey in Mrs. Benn's case.

"That would be a big help," said Dr. Emily. She measured a few white tablets into a small plastic container and wrote out some instructions. "One dose immediately, then another in a week," she told Mandy as she stuck the label onto the container. "I also want to give Indy a tonic because she is anemic, as I feared. I took some blood and her red cell count is very low." She took a bottle of liver-colored pills down from a shelf and gave it to Mandy along with the worm tablets. "I'll phone Shula now to tell her the news," she said. "And I'm going to recommend that she ask Dr. Mason for a human worm medicine for the whole family. We don't want them to be infested with roundworm, too."

Mandy made a face. "No, that really is the last thing they need."

She put Indy's medicine into her pockets and went to the shed in the backyard to get her bike. James's battered bicycle was still there, its front wheel twisted out of shape. Mr. Hunter had promised to come by in the car so that he and James could fix it. *Poor James*, thought Mandy, wheeling her bike out the door. *He'll have to walk everywhere until his bike is fixed.*

Arriving at the Benns' house a few minutes later, she hesitated for a moment before ringing the bell. Chloe had been really annoyed with her earlier. *She'll probably be even more mad at me when I start telling her how she has to treat her puppy*, Mandy thought.

Mrs. Benn came to the door. "It's so kind of you and your mom to go to all this trouble for us," she said, showing Mandy inside.

They went into the kitchen, where Indy was curled up in her basket next to the radiator, as usual. Harvey was sitting at the table drawing a picture.

"I'll tell Chloe you're here," said Mrs. Benn and she went out of the room.

Mandy was itching to give the puppy the first dose of wormer right away, or at least to pick her up and cuddle her, but she knew that Chloe would probably say she was interfering. So she looked over Harvey's shoulder and said, "That looks like your garage."

He had drawn a row of rainbow-colored ovals with tiny black circles underneath. They were lined up in front of what could have been either a gas station or a low, narrow house.

Harvey grinned up at her. "Yes, this is the garage." He pointed to the boxy-looking building, then to the oval shapes. "And all these cars have run out of gas. Just like Indy and me."

"Well, we're going to make sure Indy is back on her feet soon," Mandy said, and she went over to kneel down next to the sleeping spaniel.

Indy must have sensed Mandy's presence because she opened her eyes. She blinked a few times as if she was trying to focus, then stared at Mandy without making any attempt to get up.

"You feel rotten, don't you?" Mandy said softly, reaching out to stroke the puppy's silky head.

"Have you got some pretend gas for her, too?" asked Harvey.

"Yup. Right here in my pockets," Mandy told him. She took out the two containers and showed them to him.

Harvey made a face. "Do they taste yucky like my medicine?"

"Probably," Mandy said just as Chloe came into the kitchen. "Oh, hi there." Mandy tried to sound friendly but her heart had started beating faster and she felt her cheeks go red as she remembered their quarrel. "Er, I've brought Indy some medicine," she said awkwardly, waiting for Chloe to get angry again.

But Chloe just looked upset. "So I guess she really *is* ill," she said, then to Mandy's surprise she burst into tears and ran out of the room, brushing past her mom, who was coming back into the kitchen.

This time Mandy went after Chloe. She found her in the living room, hugging a pillow with tears pouring down her face.

"I didn't mean to upset you," Mandy began. "It's just that . . ."

"I know, I know," said Chloe, wiping her cheeks. "You

couldn't sit by and watch Indy getting worse without doing something."

Mandy nodded. "It's OK, though. We know what's wrong with her now so we can make her better."

Chloe's face crumpled. "It's all so awful," she sobbed. "First Harvey and now Indy. We were so worried about Harvey and then when Indy started looking sick, I just couldn't handle it."

Mandy suddenly realized why Chloe had seemed so indifferent toward Indy. It wasn't that she didn't care about her Christmas pup. Just the opposite, in fact. She couldn't face the fact that both her brother and her precious little puppy were sick.

Mandy put her hand on Chloe's arm and tried to comfort her. "Indy's going to be OK," she said.

"I thought you said she was really ill." Chloe sniffed.

"She is," Mandy admitted. "But she can be treated."

"So it's not too late?"

"No. Look, I've brought the medicine with me. If you like, I'll help you to give her the first dose right now," Mandy offered.

Chloe flopped down on the sofa. "I bet she'll hate it," she said. "It's bad enough trying to get her to eat, let alone take pills and things."

Mandy shrugged. "Don't worry about her appetite. That'll come back as soon as she starts feeling better.

And as for giving her the pill, we'll get around that somehow."

"Just like you did with Harvey," remarked Chloe and, for the first time in a long while, she broke into a smile.

"Except that I don't think Indy will be taken in by the gas story." Mandy grinned, then added more seriously, "Usually, we hide a pill in a piece of meat or cheese, but if Indy's not too interested in food at the moment that probably won't work. So I'll show you how to open her mouth and pop the pill into the back of her throat."

There was a tiny scrabbling sound behind them and when Mandy looked around, she saw Indy walking unsteadily into the living room. "You've woken up," Mandy said, crouching down and clapping her hands together softly to encourage the puppy to come to her. She was surprised that Indy had the energy to leave her basket.

But Indy didn't look at Mandy. She was heading straight for Chloe.

"Come on, my little angel," said Chloe, leaning down from the sofa.

Even though she must have been feeling weak and dizzy, Indy trotted over to Chloe; then, standing on her hind legs, she put her front paws on the sofa and tried to haul herself up.

Chloe scooped her up and put her on her lap. "I'm sorry I ignored how bad you were feeling," she whispered, stroking Indy's ears, which spread like gold velvet over her knees. "I'm going to make sure you get strong again really soon."

Mandy felt a lump in her throat as Indy gazed into Chloe's eyes. It was as if she was saying, *It's all right. I know you will. You're my owner and I'll never give up on you.*

The next time Mandy saw Chloe and Indy was at the fair two days later. They were coming into the crowded village hall with Sergeant and Mrs. Benn and Harvey. Indy was on her lead, trotting at Chloe's side.

"Look who's arrived," Mandy said to James, who was buying a Santa hat from Grandpa Hope's stall.

James pulled on the red felt hat. It looked several sizes too big because it slipped straight down his forehead, almost covering his eyes. "Let's go say hello," he said.

Mandy wrinkled her nose at him and chuckled. "You look more like a clown than Santa Claus in that hat," she teased as they threaded their way through the crowds. "I wouldn't be surprised if Indy starts barking at you."

But as soon as the spaniel spotted them coming toward her, she began to wag her tail. Harvey saw them at the same time, too, and he broke into a broad grin as he pulled on a smaller Santa hat. "Snap!" he said to James.

Mandy could see at once that both Indy and Harvey felt a whole lot better. Their eyes were stretched wide as if they were trying to take in everything at once: the sparkling tinsel draped around the door and window frames; the huge Christmas tree standing in the middle of the stage, its dozens of lights flashing off and on; the stalls selling everything ranging from mince pies and punch to musical Santas; and the tables where contestants could win small prizes for hooking ducks and fishing parcels out of tubs of bran.

"Hey! You two look like new!" Mandy exclaimed, glancing from Harvey to Indy.

"That's because we've been taking our medicine," said Harvey, pulling his Santa hat down his forehead so that he looked even more like James. "But Indy didn't want to at first."

"Just like you." His mom chuckled.

"I showed her how," said Harvey, sounding important. "She watched me swallow my medicine in one gulp, like a very brave boy."

Chloe moved closer to Mandy and said softly, "Actually, Indy takes her medicine because I do exactly what you showed me. I open her mouth with one hand and pop the pill right into the back of her throat."

"Well done!" Mandy whispered back warmly.

Harvey was still set on taking the credit for Indy's co-operation. "And now Indy takes her medicine when I do."

An alarm bell rang in Mandy's head. "You're not worming her every day?" she asked Chloe. Indy wasn't due for the second dose until next week.

"No, of course not." Chloe smiled. "It's just the tonic your mom gave us to give her."

"Of course," Mandy said. "I'd forgotten about that."

Indy began to jump up at James, looking more lively than any day since she first bounced out of the gift-wrapped box.

"I've said hello to you already, little one," said James, patting her head.

But Indy kept leaping up at him until Mandy guessed what the puppy wanted. "She's after whatever's in your pocket." She laughed.

"Crumbs!" said James, and he meant it literally be-cause he put his hand in his pocket and brought out some crushed dog biscuits that looked as if they'd been through the washing machine. "She's got a memory like an elephant." He chuckled, bending down to let Indy lick the crumbs out of the palm of his hand. "It was days ago when she saw me take a treat out of my pocket."

"And she eats enough to keep an elephant going, too!" Mrs. Benn protested, though her voice was full of humor.

This was all Mandy needed to hear to know that Indy was well on her way to recovery. She crouched down and patted the little spaniel, who kept still for a fraction of a second, then whirled around and sniffed at James's pockets again before leaping up at the legs of someone going past.

"No, Indy. Down!" said Chloe, grabbing the puppy. It was Mrs. Ponsonby of all people.

But the damage was already done. Indy's claws left long pale ladders in Mrs. Ponsonby's stockings.

"Oh, I'm so sorry. . . ." Chloe started to apologize.

But to Mandy's amazement Mrs. Ponsonby didn't seem at all put out. "My! What a gorgeous little spaniel," she boomed out so that half the people in the hall turned to look at Indy.

"Isn't she an absolute darling?" said Helena Dixon, who lived in the Old Vicarage.

Several others came over to make a fuss over Indy and admire her golden coat. Chloe beamed with pride. Her puppy had turned out to be one of the chief attractions at the fair!

"Even Jigsaw and Puzzle aren't getting that much attention," Mandy said with a chuckle to James as they went over to Dr. Mason's popular "Rat Challenge" stall. A big sign that read WHICH RAT'S THAT? stood next to a complicated course of colored tubes. People could win toffees if they guessed which tunnel the doctor's beloved pets would eventually come out of.

Mandy was both pleased and surprised to see how well-attended the stall was. With the bad publicity that rats usually received, she'd expected it to be deserted. Instead, the group that had gathered in front of the stand seemed fascinated by the handsome rodents and cheered whenever the pair emerged from a tunnel.

Dr. Mason was collecting people's money when he glanced across and caught Mandy's eye. "Doing well for themselves, aren't they?" he said.

Mandy nodded and he continued, "I knew they'd soon make friends once people saw how clever they are."

Harvey managed to push his way to the front and, handing Dr. Mason a coin, pointed to a tunnel. "They'll come out of this green one," he predicted as the doctor released Jigsaw and Puzzle at the beginning of the maze again.

Moments later, the sleek-coated pair popped out of the tunnel Harvey had chosen, one after the other. He jumped up and down in delight. "I won!"

"There must be something extra in that yellow medicine!" Dr. Mason laughed, giving Harvey a foil-wrapped toffee. He looked at Mrs. Benn. "Is everything going smoothly?"

"No trouble at all." Mrs. Benn smiled. "Antibiotics, wormer — it all gets swallowed without a peep. All thanks to Mandy's gas game, and to Indy, of course. Harvey and that pup are the best of friends. It's almost as if Harvey's competing with her to see who's the bravest patient."

"Not to mention who can run faster, eat more, play rough-and-tumble more roughly, jump higher. . . ." Sergeant Benn tailed off and shook his head. "It's like a madhouse in our place these days."

"And here, too." Mandy laughed, pointing to Indy, who was charging around the rats' table. "It's just as well she can't get up to join them."

Chloe's eyes widened and she put her hand over her mouth. "Oops!" she said, lunging forward to grab Indy, who wriggled and squirmed, trying to escape.

"You're not going anywhere." Chloe laughed. Catching Mandy's eye, she added, "She's a real handful now that she's back to normal."

"Now you know what it's like being a dog owner," said James with a grin. "You've got to remind them all the time who the boss is."

"Well, we know who that is in our house, don't we, Chloe?" said Mrs. Benn so that Mandy guessed it was Indy who was in charge of everyone and, because of her shaky start, was getting away with all sorts of things.

"You'll have to start teaching her some manners," Mandy suggested to Chloe, trying to sound tactful.

"I'm trying," replied Chloe. "But it's very hard, you know. It's like her tummy is full of jumping beans that make her do crazy things!"

Gran had been going around the hall persuading people to buy her raffle tickets. Now she came over to Chloe. "I don't think you've taken a ticket yet, have you?"

"No, I haven't," said Chloe. She looked at her dad. "Can I buy one, please?"

Sergeant Benn gave her a handful of coins. "We'll go halves if you win a prize." He grinned.

"It's a deal," Chloe agreed and she wrote her name down in one of the few gaps left on the raffle sheet.

Gran persuaded Mrs. Ponsonby and Dr. Adam to buy the last few tickets before she announced that it was time to draw the raffle. She went up to the stage and banged an old brass gong. "I need someone to draw the winning tickets." She scanned the hall until her eyes fell on Harvey. "Ah! Just the person I'm looking for. Harvey Benn! Would you like to pull out the winning tickets?"

Harvey didn't need asking twice. He wriggled through the crowd and climbed up the stairs onto the stage. Gran held a big glass bowl in front of him and told him to close his eyes and choose a ticket.

Looking very important, Harvey pulled out the first number.

"This is for Ernie's carpentry skills," said Gran, consulting her list of prizes. She took the slip of paper from Harvey and unfolded it. "B 7," she announced, then checked another list to see who had taken that ticket. "Walter Pickard!"

"I don't believe it." Walter laughed. He called across the hall to Ernie, "I know just what I need. A new scratching post for Flicker, please!" Flicker was his newest cat. He'd given her a home not long ago after she'd been washed down the river and rescued by Mandy during a flood.

"You'll have it within the week," Ernie promised.

"The next prize is James's computer lessons," said Gran. She took the ticket that Harvey had drawn out of the bowl and paused as she looked down at her list again. Her eyes widened when she saw who the winner was, then she broke into helpless laughter.

"Who is it?" someone called.

Gran tried to say the name of the winner, but she was laughing so much that she had to beckon Mandy onstage so that she could read out the name.

"Oh, this is fantastic!" Mandy exclaimed when she saw who it was. She looked around the hall for the face she knew so well and when she found it, she announced triumphantly, "And the winner is . . . Tom Hope!"

"Me?" Grandpa's hand flew to his chest. Recovering quickly from his surprise, he protested, "And what do I want computer lessons for?" He sounded indignant, but Mandy could tell that he was secretly pleased to have the chance to come face-to-face with modern technology at last. "You'd better be a patient teacher, young James," he said gruffly. "You know what they say about old dogs and new tricks!"

When it was time to choose the winner for the chocolates, Mandy held her breath. James really deserved to win them after all the work he'd done on the raffle.

"Mrs. McFarlane's giant box of chocolates goes to . . ." Gran looked at her list.

Let it be James. Let it be James, Mandy willed silently.

"Harvey Benn," announced Gran.

The little boy was already fishing around for the next winner so it took a moment for the news to sink in. "Is that me?" he suddenly said, opening his eyes.

"Yes. Unless there's another Harvey Benn in the hall." Gran chuckled.

"But we didn't buy him a ticket," Mrs. Benn frowned.

"Well, someone did," said Gran. She put down the bowl of tickets, then picked up the chocolates and gave them to Harvey.

The enormous box almost dwarfed the little boy, who was grinning too broadly to say anything.

Mandy wondered who the mystery ticket buyer was. She glanced at James to see how he felt about not winning the coveted chocolates. His ears were bright red, and Mandy suddenly knew without any doubt that he was responsible for the unexpected prize. James had

probably put every single ticket he'd bought into Harvey's name! She gave him a thumbs-up and he put his finger to his lips, signaling to her not to say a word to anyone.

With the chocolates in his mother's safekeeping, Harvey went back to the task of drawing out the winners' names. Among them was Reverend Hadcroft, whose prize was Emily Hope's offer of a car wash. "But I haven't got a car," he pointed out. "Only my old bicycle."

"Never mind, I'll give that a good wash, then." Dr. Emily laughed.

Another prize also revolved around a bicycle. It was Bill Ward's promise to repair or service anyone's bike.

"And that goes to James Hunter," declared Gran, so that Mandy started to wonder if some invisible forces were at work, deciding who won the raffle prizes.

"It's just what you needed," she told James, who had come to stand on the stage with her. "How lucky is that?"

James nodded in amazement. "And to think I had just as much chance of winning the sewing lessons! If I didn't know better, I'd say the whole thing had been rigged."

And when the winner of Adam Hope's offer to clean out a garage turned out to be Dr. Adam himself, whose garage needed tidying the most of anyone in Welford, James had to concede that maybe, just maybe, a mischievous power was at work.

Finally, Gran announced that there was just one more prize. "It came in at the last minute," she said, holding up an unmarked envelope.

"What is it?" asked Reverend Hadcroft.

"We'll find out once we know who the winner is," said Gran, and she held the tickets in front of Harvey again.

The little boy closed his eyes and dipped his hand into the bowl. He swished the slips of paper around until he settled on one. "Here," he said, pulling it out.

"Let me see," said Gran, matching the number with the name on the list. A wide smile spread across her face and she looked at the expectant audience. "Our last winner," she said, taking off her glasses, "is Chloe Benn."

"Oh, wow!" exclaimed Chloe. She made her way onto the stage with Indy tumbling along at her side. Mandy bent down to pat the puppy and realized that her tummy was no longer bloated, and her ribs could only just be felt beneath her thick, glossy fur.

There was hardly a sound in the hall as Chloe opened the envelope. Inside was a piece of paper with something written on it. "I don't believe it!" Chloe said breathlessly, reading the note.

Mandy couldn't bear the suspense any longer. "What is it?" she asked.

Chloe looked at her with her eyes shining. "It's a puppy training course!" she exclaimed. She looked down at Indy. "We're going to school, little girl!"

Mandy was astonished. So many coincidences in one evening! Then she saw Gran and Grandpa exchange a wink, and she realized that Chloe's prize wasn't a coincidence after all. In this case at least, there had been some crafty intervention by her grandparents. She knew they'd been worried to hear how sick Indy was, and they were obviously determined that this particular pup was going to be loved and cherished for a long time yet. They must have organized the prize and somehow made sure that Chloe won it.

Sergeant Benn was making his way through the crowd to the front of the hall. "Police! Move aside," he joked. Climbing onto the stage, he said to Chloe, "I've come to claim my half of the prize, since I paid for the ticket."

"Well, it's not quite the same as Harvey's chocolates, which could be shared," Chloe pointed out, looking worried.

"No, but I think I should come to school with you and Indy," said Sergeant Benn, with his eyes twinkling. He smiled down at the puppy.

"Now that *is* good news," came Mrs. Benn's voice. "The more of us who can keep that rascal under control, the better."

Chloe bent down and picked up Indy. She hugged the little dog close to her and kissed the top of her head. "You're going to be the best-behaved dog in Welford," she promised. "And we're going to have tons of fun at puppy school."

As if she was agreeing with her, Indy looked up at Chloe and licked her cheek.

James nudged Mandy with his elbow. "I don't think the novelty of having a puppy has worn off after all," he said quietly. "It looks like Chloe's more over the moon about Indy now than when she first opened her present the other day."

"Oh, yes," Mandy said happily. She was completely certain now that Indy wasn't just for Christmas. "She's a dog for life."

Read all the Animal Ark books!

by Ben M. Baglio

- ❏ BDB 0-439-09700-2 **Bunnies in the Bathroom**
- ❏ BDB 0-439-34407-7 **Cat in a Crypt**
- ❏ BDB 0-439-34393-3 **Cats at the Campground**
- ❏ BDB 0-439-34413-1 **Colt in the Cave**
- ❏ BDB 0-439-34386-0 **Dog at the Door**
- ❏ BDB 0-439-34408-5 **Dog in the Dungeon**
- ❏ BDB 0-439-23021-7 **Dolphin in the Deep**
- ❏ BDB 0-439-34415-8 **Foal in the Fog**
- ❏ BDB 0-439-34385-2 **Foals in the Field**
- ❏ BDB 0-439-23018-7 **Guinea Pig in the Garage**
- ❏ BDB 0-439-09701-0 **Hamster in a Handbasket**
- ❏ BDB 0-439-34387-9 **Horse in the House**
- ❏ BDB 0-439-44891-3 **Hound at the Hospital**
- ❏ BDB 0-439-44897-2 **Hound on the Heath**
- ❏ BDB 0-439-68758-6 **Kitten in the Candy Corn**
- ❏ BDB 0-439-09698-7 **Kitten in the Cold**

- ❏ BDB 0-590-18749-X **Kittens in the Kitchen**
- ❏ BDB 0-439-68488-9 **Labrador on the Lawn**
- ❏ BDB 0-439-34392-5 **Mare in the Meadow**
- ❏ BDB 0-590-66231-7 **Ponies at the Point**
- ❏ BDB 0-439-34388-7 **Pony in a Package**
- ❏ BDB 0-590-18750-3 **Pony on the Porch**
- ❏ BDB 0-439-34391-7 **Pup at the Palace**
- ❏ BDB 0-590-18751-1 **Puppies in the Pantry**
- ❏ BDB 0-439-34389-5 **Puppy in a Puddle**
- ❏ BDB 0-439-68496-X **Racehorse in the Rain**
- ❏ BDB 0-590-18757-0 **Sheepdog in the Snow**
- ❏ BDB 0-439-68757-8 **Siamese in the Sun**
- ❏ BDB 0-439-34126-4 **Stallion in the Storm**
- ❏ BDB 0-439-34390-9 **Tabby in the Tub**
- ❏ BDB 0-439-44892-1 **Terrier in the Tinsel**

Available wherever you buy books, or use this order form.

Scholastic Inc., P.O. Box 7502, Jefferson City, MO 65102

Please send me the books I have checked above. I am enclosing $_____ (please add $2.00 to cover shipping and handling). Send check or money order—no cash or C.O.D.s please.

Name _____ Age _____

Address _____

City _____ State/Zip _____

Please allow four to six weeks for delivery. Offer good in the U.S. only. Sorry, mail orders are not available to residents of Canada. Prices subject to change.

ABBL08